Always Love

Suzanne M.Hurley

A Wings ePress, Inc.
Inspirational Novel

Wings ePress, Inc.

Edited by: Jeanne Smith
Copy Edited by: Joan C. Powell
Executive Editor: Jeanne Smith
Cover Artist: Trisha FitzGerald-Jung

All rights reserved

Wings ePress Books
www.wingsepress.com

Copyright © 2020 by: Suzanne M. Hurley
ISBN-13: 978-1-61309-588-1
ISBN-10: 1-61309-588-0

Published In the United States Of America

Wings ePress Inc.
3000 N. Rock Road
Newton, KS 67114

Dedication

I dedicate this book to everyone on the journey to living their true, authentic selves. May they be brave, strong, and courageous as they seek their own truth and peace.

To Mary Lou, who truly lives an authentic life and touches the heart of everyone she meets with her grace, compassion and love. Thank you for your continual guidance.

To my family, and to Sheila, Theresa, Dorothy, Marja and Lynda for your constant support.

To John for being a terrific sounding board.

To my dog, Rico, for being the best companion a girl could have.

To Trisha Fitzgerald who designed the cover, and the entire Wings' staff for their dedication and hard work.

And to Kathy Zadvorny for allowing me to experience the beauty of caterpillars emerging as butterflies.

* * *

Prologue

Fascinated, forty-two-year-old Jenna Evans eyed a tiny caterpillar crawling across the deck. The sun lit up its cream, black, and golden stripes, enriching them, creating a glow, then suddenly—poof!—it burst into a tiny ball of fire with legs. It wasn't really on fire. It was all an illusion of bright shiny rays bouncing off glossy colors and was actually quite spectacular.

Or maybe it was the wine that distorted the little creature.

How many glasses had she downed?

She glanced at the bottle. Only a quarter gone. She wasn't even aware she'd had that much.

Nevertheless, she was captivated by the little bug. Or was it an insect? She couldn't quite remember.

She took another sip. Then another...

Words she'd heard an hour ago shot out, slamming into her thoughts, upsetting her all over again.

"Sorry, Jenna," said James Hull. *"I know I promised you a partnership, but it won't happen now. My son is coming home to take over the law practice. Hope you don't mind."*

Yeah, she did mind. A lot.

Don't think about this.

It hurt her heart way too much, not to mention her head, where a migraine pounded away.

Thump, thump, thump.

Just watch the caterpillar.

Her life was so busy, she rarely had a moment to allow her thoughts to wander, let alone even notice a caterpillar, or any crawly creature for that matter. Except spiders. Okay, a spider wasn't an insect but an arachnid, and she couldn't stand them. She always managed to notice the leggy creatures, even in the most obscure places. It was as if they haunted her. Much like today's events.

"So, no partnership? But do I still have a job?" she had asked.

Hull's downcast eyes spoke volumes.

She shook her head, trying to forget.

But she couldn't.

Life had been one constant battle since she had gone back to work full-time three years earlier, determined to make partner, a dream of hers practically from birth. She'd gone from being a kid representing troubled friends by advocating on their behalf to their parents, to joining the debate club in high school, and finally reveling in the honor of being accepted at law school. Nothing made her happier than fighting for a cause and winning, especially if it bettered the world.

Then along came a husband, children, and her priorities changed.

She'd been a stay-at-home mom for a good long while, raising her children, - along with her husband. In many ways, her spouse was her third child. He was a brilliant man but forgetful and she found she had to keep after him about a lot of day-to-day life occurrences, such as reminding him of his doctor/dentist appointments, driving forgotten lunches to his workplace, and picking up his dry-cleaned suits. Still, she'd always managed to squeeze in part-time work for the law firm where she'd started working, when first called to the bar and becoming a fully licensed lawyer. Her boss was grooming her to take over, or at least he had led her to believe that, constantly talking about how the firm's shingle would one day read James Hull and Jenna Evans. Eventually, just Jenna Evans.

Bam.

It was all over. Finished. Done.

"You mean, you're firing me?"

"Of course, I'm not firing you. It's just I'm not sure I have enough work for three lawyers. This is a small town."

"So, you're laying me off? I really have lost my job?"

Hull had turned his head toward the window, making it obvious he did not want to look right at her. She had gotten her answer.

She had stood, held her head high in a futile show of dignity, and walked out of his office. After all the work she had done for this man, she refused to beg for her job, or let him see how upset she was.

Instantly feeling sick to her stomach, sucker-punched, shaken to the core, she'd grabbed her purse, left the building, got into her SUV and headed home.

Now she was out on her deck with a bottle of wine. The kids wouldn't be arriving until much later and by then she'd be sobered up on coffee. She really wasn't much of a drinker and she'd make sure she didn't overdo the booze. Her children and her husband deserved a clear-headed wife and mother, not someone who turned to alcohol to help her cope.

Which she did.

Not usually, but at least at this moment.

It was just that she needed to forget the pain slicing through her. For a while. Until she gathered her wits about her.

Wait a second.

She stared at the caterpillar again. It appeared to be carrying something.

Did it really have an object in its mouth?

Intrigued, she put down her wine glass, jumped off her chair and got down on her hands and knees to get a better view.

Yes, something was there.

She crept along, keeping to the rhythm of the tiny crawler, checking it out.

"What do you have? What are you carrying?"

She started to giggle.

If anyone saw a grown woman in a black power suit crawling on the deck, talking to a caterpillar, she'd be locked up for good. They'd think she'd lost it. But it sure was a nice diversion. Something to focus on rather than legal briefs, a form to fill out, or the disappointing looks on her husband and children's faces when she had to stay late at work, or forgot something, or wasn't as pleasant as she should be. Just couldn't help it all. She was stressed out most of the time.

Besides, she liked caterpillars. As a matter of fact she loved all of nature's miracles, both animal and plant-based. Okay, she did have a thing about spiders, but she would never ever hurt any of them. Maybe one day she'd even grow to like them. After all, their cobweb creations were absolutely beautiful.

Once upon a time, she had always imagined she'd be living on a farm with all sorts of chickens and horses and cows. And dogs. Oh, how she loved dogs. And of course cats, too.

And caterpillars.

Her husband used to tease her about her affinity for caterpillars.

They're not the nicest things to look at, he used to say, flicking them off the garden hose.

And they manage to get into and onto everything, especially just where we don't want them.

If he had seen this little caterpillar on the deck, he'd be looking to get rid of it pronto.

"But they turn into magnificent, gorgeous butterflies," she'd fired back. *"And then they can soar into the skies, free as anything."*

The ability to change, to metamorphose, to be all you could be, was something she admired enormously.

She felt lucky that this little caterpillar came along at an exact time of need and gave her something to think about, especially since everything in her life had changed in a moment.

A flash.

At least when it came to her dream job.

Sigh.

Life seemed such a mess. Like a skein of tangled wool tied in knots her granny used to make her unravel when knitting her latest creation.

At least back then she'd had success, forming a beautiful ball of neatly wrapped yarn, and presenting it back all ready to use again.

Today was a complete failure, for no way could she manage to undo her present situation. Looked like it would remain tangled forever.

Her life was always filled with demands.

With work. With family. With just about anything and everything.

And now she didn't even have a job. One she had loved and had wanted desperately.

Forget about all that.

At least for now.

She finally managed to get a good look at what was in the little creature's mouth. Why it was a tiny green leaf all rolled up. Supper, maybe?

"Hey, little one," she said, figuring this was more respectful than saying, 'it'. She actually felt bad thinking of the creature as an 'it', but since she didn't know if it was a boy or girl, 'it' would have to do. At least in her private thoughts.

"Where are you going in such a hurry?"

Of course, the wee one didn't answer.

She giggled again.

Did she really expect it to? As far as she knew, caterpillars didn't talk. Or answer questions.

How silly. Ridiculous, actually.

Um, how much wine had she downed now? She glanced at the bottle, checking again. Still not a lot. She shouldn't be feeling the effects yet, or at all.

Oh well, didn't mean she couldn't talk to an insect. There were no rules that said you couldn't chat with crawly things. She used to do it all the time as a child. After all, people talked to their pets and she knew some who even conversed with plants. Not a thing wrong with her behavior. Just curiosity and a diversion from her sad thoughts.

Wait a second.

Did the caterpillar glance at her?

She knew from science class way back in elementary school that they had twelve eyes, and she was pretty sure at least one of them turned her way, if not two.

Science class.

Oh, how she loved learning everything she could there. In fact, it was surprising that she went into law and not science, although she'd often thought of becoming an environmental lawyer, fighting to preserve the environment and all-natural resources.

Wait.

There it was again. She wasn't imagining it one bit. The caterpillar really was looking at her. Three eyes were staring at her. Now, four.

She stared back.

They were big, intelligent-looking, and completely mesmerizing. What? Were they blue? Really? Can a caterpillar have blue eyes? Or was it the sunlight making it appear so?

"You're so beautiful. Do you know that? Did anyone ever tell you that?" she crooned.

Whoa!

Did the creature actually smile? Had it heard her?

As far as she knew, they had no ears.

Like, really?

Sure looked like a grin to her.

She stopped for a second to rub her eyes.

Was the wine affecting her so much she was seeing things?

Couldn't be. It was too early for that.

She opened them again. The caterpillar had stopped, as well.

Yep, it really was looking at her. With all twelve eyes now. And yes, they were blue.

Real or not, too bad, this was fun. It was as if she were some kind of caterpillar-whisperer and was making a huge connection with this one.

A caterpillar whisperer. She liked the sound of that. Maybe she should start raising them, watching them emerge as butterflies and then setting them free. She'd love that. She could feel her eyes shining at the thought of a new venture, when all of a sudden it swung its head away and started moving fast again. Hurrying to keep up, she jumped to her feet, following as it made a quick turn and crawled up to the top of the railing around the deck.

"Where are you going? You look like you're actually following some kind of path."

Once again, Jenna thought an eye turned her way.

She was sure it really was watching her again, as one more looked her way. Then another. Yikes. Did it wink? Were all twelve winking at her?

It was just for a split second, before the caterpillar turned and crawled along the railing to a branch, hopped on it, heading toward the big maple tree that grew alongside the deck.

It disappeared into a maze of leaves.

Sadness swarmed her as she shouted out, "Bye, little cutie. Enjoy your supper."

She already missed the sweet caterpillar with the big eyes who she seemed to have connected with. She missed the distraction.

Pain seeped in again, stealing her brief moment of solace.

She dropped down on her hands and knees and curled up into a tiny little ball, trying to make herself as small as could be. She glanced at her watch. She needed to make some coffee. Soon her husband and kids would be home and duty would call but she was secretly hoping that maybe they wouldn't notice her out here hiding in the corner behind the chairs.

She wanted to stay right there.

At least for a while.

She wanted more time.

For herself.

She wasn't really drunk, so caffeine could wait.

She was tired, so darn tired and fed up with trying to make her life work. And, as it turned out, all for nothing. She was obviously a lousy lawyer or Hull would have fought to keep her. Added to this, she wasn't that great of a mom or wife, for that matter. Work had claimed her and now the dreams she'd pursued had popped like balloons and drifted down, lost, hidden, trampled in the dirt, nowhere to be found.

Life had been kind of good for a while.

She was, or at least had been, a full-time lawyer in a law firm, while her husband was the principal of the local high school.

Both fulfilling their hopes and wishes.

Then, time took over and cracks appeared. Tense, unruly, hurtful cracks.

What was now so ironic was that her whole family had made sacrifices when she went back to work so she could fulfill her dream. She loved criminal law, especially helping the underdog, and had been anxious to work full-time again. Her husband's wishes had come true, he had risen to become the head of the local high school, her children were doing well and she had felt it was time to immerse herself back into law full strength. She thought it was good role modeling for her son and daughter, to see their mother following her heart, reaching for the stars, doing what she always told them to do. So surprisingly, as well as incredibly touching, after expressing her hopes to her family, they had been incredibly supportive, offering to help as much as they could. Especially her husband.

Her husband.

Scott.

Sigh.

Despite his support and all sorts of good intentions, lately they seemed to have grown apart. The cracks she'd thought of earlier, if she were completely honest, were more like deep abysses. She knew a lot of couples felt the same, but she had vowed they never would. She had always felt it was Jenna and Scott forever, and she was determined to keep their love alive and thriving.

Yeah, right.

She couldn't do it. Not alone. And her husband seemed too busy to even talk to her anymore. But she couldn't blame him; she was the exact same. They were both in a rush all the time. There always seemed to be one conflict after another, daily schedules to follow, and endless errands to perform. Their carefully orchestrated date nights to keep their love alive had ended, habitual hello and goodbye kisses stopped, and intimacy was a thing of the past.

When was the last time they made love?

She couldn't even begin to pin it down; it'd been so long.

And then there were her children.

Two of them.

Her daughter Ellie was in grade nine; her son Jason in grade six. She never felt she had enough time for them, either. Not anymore. Especially her daughter. Her son always seemed well-adjusted and happy, immersed in sports and studies. However, Ellie was another matter. High school could be tough, especially when your dad was the principal, and lately their daughter seemed withdrawn. *"I'm fine,"* was her favorite answer as she stormed off to her room, slamming her door, not wanting to talk.

No one wanted to communicate.

No one wanted to spend time together.

The kids stayed in their rooms...her husband in the den and she at a desk in the bedroom.

Seemed like they all lived separate lives.

Jenna rocked back and forth.

She was exhausted from trying to hold it all together, striving to be the perfect wife, mother and lawyer.

And to think now she'd lost her job. Next could be Scott, and even her children.

She was such a failure.

Buried under endless duties. Doing much, achieving little.

She stared up at the heavens.

"God, are you up there? Please? Are you listening?"

Pause.

What was she expecting? A lightning bolt? A vision?

She tried again.

"Can you help me? Er, that is, if you have time?"

He probably was way too busy anyway.

Or maybe too tired.

She figured God could be just simply too worn out to give her much notice. After all, there were way more people in greater pain than she was—struggling at war, living day to day with no money, never knowing if they would even see food again.

Jenna used to be into God at one point in her life, for her parents had raised her to believe.

She had once wanted to become a missionary and fly off to poorer countries to help build houses and schools. She used to even run a fundraiser at whatever school she attended at the time —a bake sale— to raise money to help those less fortunate than she was. One time she brought in over five thousand dollars and spread it to five different charities. She felt she was really doing something to help the world, to leave it a better place.

But for a long time, her beliefs had all drifted away as well.

She knew her mom always told her to pray more when she was busy, asking for help, but she felt she was just too preoccupied, too tired, and to be even more honest, couldn't be bothered to do that.

Truth be told, she never even gave God a thought these days.

Except for today.

And God was silent.

Couldn't say she blamed him though. Since she was pretty silent when it came to her faith, how could she even expect Him to help?

Sigh.

"Sure wish I could join that caterpillar right about now. Wish I were anywhere else but here."

Okay, she was talking out loud again, but she just didn't care. So what if someone heard her?

"Lock me away. I deserve it. Life sucks, anyway. Sure I'd miss my children and my husband, but they would probably be better off without me. I'm such a loser."

Now how sad that she thought such a thing.

But she'd been so grumpy these days, she even hated being around herself, but obviously had no choice in *that* matter.

Oh, stop thinking. My head hurts even more.

Hey, maybe I should check to see where the crawly one was. Maybe I could still see the little fireball. It would make her happy watching it plod along, obviously with some kind of agenda, probably a whole lot better than her current one. She didn't even have one, so anyone else's was better than hers.

"Where are you, little one?" she asked, scanning the tree.

Was that it?

She was sure she saw a glimpse of something moving. Slowly, but surely. Oh, good. She really needed more diversions and the delightful wonder of having twelve eyes winking at her seemed to help. Blue ones, at that.

She had an idea.

Jumping up, she kicked off her heels and climbed up on the railing, balancing herself on the wide plank. She'd been a gymnast as a kid and always had perfect balance. Something she was proud of.

She leaned way over, hoping to get a better view of the little creature.

"Where are you?" she screamed. "I need you."

Oops!

One

Wait! What?

Jenna heard voices.

Dim. Faint. Definitely there.

Lots of weird noises, too. Hums, clangs, whirs, creaks...

It was abrupt, harsh, pulling her out of her deep relaxing sleep.

Awww...I don't want to wake up.

Wait a second. Was that her husband talking? Her kids?

Were they right here with her? Had they found her hiding place out on the deck?

Darn.

They sounded shocked, scared, nervous, annoyed even.

Why?

Were they fighting? Angry at her? Giving her errands to do?

Had she missed a commitment? Something she was supposed to do and just forgot? Sure seemed the norm, these days.

Or were they stunned to find her curled up on the deck?

She wasn't drunk; she hadn't even finished one full glass of wine.

Were they just concerned because she was out here asleep?

Oh, wait. She had lost her job. Did they know this? Had they discovered she'd walked out of her meeting with her boss? Were they worried for her?

She kept her eyes closed, listening. No way did she want to give up the peace she oozed in, just by lying there. She felt good for a change. Maybe she could just stay asleep for days or even the rest of her life. It could all just pass her by for all she cared at the moment.

She was just so tired.

The voices grew nearer and louder. She could now make out what they were saying.

"What is this?"

"Looks like a tiny girl."

"A girl?"

"Yeah, you know. A human. A girl. You see them all the time playing on swings, climbing trees, mucking in the milkweed, sometimes even messing up our homes."

"That's no girl. It's a small woman."

"A woman?"

"Yeah. She has a grownup suit on. You often see ladies wearing them with the tiny girls on the swings. Playing with them after work, I guess."

"But I've never seen one so small and what's she doing here, Shelly? And why is she little? Humans are big. Way big."

Shelly? Who is Shelly? And she was small? What the—

"Have no clue. No idea whatsoever. This is a mystery."

A mystery?

Who was out here with her? There were at least two of them.

Come to think of it, she didn't recognize the voices.

They weren't her family, that was for sure. One sounded male, but very deep and raspy, not in the least like her husband's or son's. And the female voice was higher pitched than her daughter's.

Should she look?

Nah, she didn't want to. She craved more sleep.

On the other hand, was she in some kind of danger?

Or...were her children and husband in danger too?

They really weren't expected home until later, but still...

Was this a burglary?

Would they hurt her? Her family?

Maybe it would be good to check it out.

Maybe?

Yes.

Slowly, she opened one eye.

Startled to see twelve big eyes times two staring at her, she opened her other eye and sat up fast.

"Who are you? And what are you doing in my house?" she screamed.

Jenna looked around in horror at the two strange creatures on the deck with her. One had blue eyes—twelve of them—and wore a black felt bowler hat, while the other sported a shiny sparkly pink hairband. They didn't say a word, just stared at her.

"Why you're...you're big caterpillars," she uttered in fear. "Monster caterpillars."

Frantically, she tried to remember what time of the year it was.

"It's not Halloween, so why are you dressed in costumes? Big, big costumes? Actually, it's pretty darn cool, very life-like, but scary all the same. Who are you?"

Finally, one of them opened its mouths.

"We're not big," said a female voice, coming from the caterpillar with the pink hairband. She sounded outraged. "And we're not monsters. You're just little."

"Yeah, really extra small," said the other one with the jaunty black hat.

Jenna checked out her hands, legs and feet. "No, I'm the same. You're just big." She shrieked and looked around. "Wait. Where am I? I'm not on my deck."

It appeared as if she were in some kind of cave, dark, plain, earthy and smelling mostly like mud. She had never been in a room like this before.

Had she been kidnapped?

Terrified more than ever, she stared back at them again. Unnerved by all the eyes, and not sure which ones to look at, she glanced up at the dark ceiling, or roof, or whatever it was, screaming, "Where have you taken me? You didn't hurt my family, did you?"

"No, of course not." This was spoken in unison.

She jerked her head back to face them, jumping up on her feet, hands on her hips, trying to puff up to look bigger.

"You're not going to hurt me, are you? Because I've taken karate and I'm good at it. I can bring you to your knees." She looked down at their legs and shuddered. How many knees did they actually have? Way too many.

She peeked back at them, swinging into another pose, suddenly not so brave, but faking it.

Success.

They appeared alarmed. Guess she'd scared them with her new fighting stance, legs apart, arms raised, hands curled into fists.

But just how many people were in those costumes?

She wouldn't be able to take them all on.

Could she?

"No, of course we're not going to hurt you or anyone. And you are in our home. Our guest," said the smaller caterpillar. "I'm Shelly and this here is Kirby."

"Glad to meet you, little one," said Kirby.

"Little? I repeat, I'm not little. I'm forty-two years old and five feet six inches tall. You're just big. How many of you are there? Do you have stilts inside those costumes? How do you do it?"

"Costumes?" Kirby glanced at Shelly. "What is she talking about?"

"Oh, come on," said Jenna, her shock, anger and fear changing to annoyance at this so-called charade. "Caterpillars are small. There must be five of you in each get-up. Are we at a circus? Museum? Carnival? Is this a joke? It's not April Fools' or my birthday. Or Christmas for that matter. You don't have Santa hats on. What's this all about? Is my family trying to surprise me for some reason? Cheer me up?"

"We *are* small but you're smaller. What are *you* doing here?" asked Kirby. "I just saw you on your deck a few minutes ago, when I was coming home. But you were much bigger then." He crawled closer to check her out. "Yes, it was definitely you. I remember your red curly hair tied back in that ponytail, as well as those green eyes staring at me when you crawled along beside me."

Jenna shuffled back, cowering. She did remember the little caterpillar she'd been fascinated by and had indeed crawled to take a closer look. Come to think of it, he did seem to have blue eyes but she'd eventually figured it really was just the light shining on him. Caterpillars did not have blue eyes.

"You actually saw me do that?" she asked.

"Yes. Must admit it was strange, but nice, too. You seemed so friendly. You were even talking to me."

This is ridiculous, she thought.

Had she stumbled into some kind of parallel universe where creatures talked?

Because the more she looked, they sure seemed real and not people in costumes like she'd originally thought.

Or was it a dream?

Yes, it must be some kind of weird fantasy dream.

She pinched herself.

"Ouch." That hurt.

Could you hurt yourself in dreams?

Guess so. Because she sure couldn't be sitting in some kind of cave talking to two big caterpillars who stared at her suspiciously. That would be insane. Ludicrous. Certifiable.

Or...unless it was a severe case of 'beware what you wish for.' After all, she did remember wishing she could join the caterpillar, longing to re-discover her love of nature and all its creatures. Yes, spiders too. She'd even prayed.

Holy crap.

Had God sent her here?

Was this the answer to her prayer? She liked caterpillars, so *bang* here she was? She did remember the story of the blind man in the Bible and Jesus asking him what he wanted. Of course, to all of us readers, we figured it was obvious that he wanted his sight back. But God respected this man and asked first. Okay, this wasn't exactly the same. She didn't directly tell God she wanted to live with caterpillars but she did remember praying and wanting to join the little insect.

Had it come true?

No, couldn't have.

Besides, there were no little caterpillars here. She was the small one.

It was silly to even think such a thought.

But they really did appear authentic. Like big life-like caterpillars. The real deal.

Then it hit her.

This was no answer to a prayer. Or a dream.

It was a nightmare.

Or...wait a second. Had she died? Maybe God was saying, "Surprise! Heaven is full of big insects."

She looked around.

Nah. There was no God figure scurrying around. Or wasn't it supposed to be St. Peter who met you at the pearly gates?

Or...was she in hell?

Yikes. Was there a devil figure lurking around?

Nah.

It had to be a dream. An outlandish one at that.

Or...she had been taken away somewhere by weird circus people resembling real caterpillars or something, but if these crazy creatures were looking for some kind of ransom money, they'd have to wait a long time. No way did they have that kind of dough in their bank accounts.

She inched herself back, away from them.

Could she make a run for it?

Kirby followed her.

"Behave, Kirby," said Shelly, slicing into her thoughts. "You're scaring the lady."

"Yeah, you really are," said Jenna. "You're big, you have long spooky tentacles that never seem to stop moving, too many eyes and a ton of legs. I don't know why I'm here and what you're doing with me." A tear dripped down her face and she started to shake. Just describing them out loud made it all seem so real again. Terror swarmed her. What was happening?

"There, there," said Shelly. "Don't cry."

"Yeah, please stop. You're making me cry too," said Kirby, wiping his own tears away. Obviously hard to do with twelve eyes.

"Oh, sorry," said Jenna. "I hate the idea of hurting someone. Even a creature, if that's who you are. And hey, I didn't know caterpillars could cry." She couldn't believe she was even saying such a thing. It sounded absurd. Ridiculous. Soothing a caterpillar? No way.

"Not all of them," said Shelly. "But Kirby here is one in a million. He's very sensitive. What's your name, by the way?"

Well, she might as well identify herself and play along in this bizarre world. She seemed to have no choice.

"Jenna Evans."

"Why, it's a pretty name," said Kirby.

"Thank you. I was named after my grandmother. So you really saw me on the deck, Kirby? I thought some of your eyes were watching me. Or a couple of them."

"Sure, I saw you. Thought your hair was so pretty. It was all shiny." He suddenly turned red.

Really?

Caterpillars could blush?

Guess so.

"And I thought you were beautiful," said Jenna. "Like a tiny, gorgeous fireball. Didn't know caterpillars had blue eyes, though."

"Not usually. It's rare," he said.

She glanced back and forth between them, still afraid. "Um...are you sure you're not going to hurt me?"

"Promise," said Kirby and Shelly together.

"I was more worried you might hurt *us*," said Kirby. "After all, you somehow followed me here. Are there more arriving later?" He scanned the room.

"No, no. Just me. But hey, that's another thing I don't understand. I *didn't* follow you and besides, where is here? Where am I? A cave somewhere? I live in Caledonia, Ontario. I didn't even know there were caves here."

"No cave. You're in Milkweed Manor."

"What? Milkweed. I'm in a weed?"

Relaxing her stance, she ran over to a hole in the wall and leaned her head out. Yep, this was milkweed. She recognized the plant that grew along the edge of her front yard. Except it was huge. Really, really big. She swung her head back, glaring at the caterpillars, shocked.

"I really am in a weed? The stem of a drab, horrible, old, smelly weed?"

"Don't be so rude," said Shelly. "Nothing drab or horrible about the place. This is our home and we love it here."

She sounded annoyed, not to mention insulted.

"Oh, sorry. Now I've hurt you and I'm not like that at all. This is really quite lovely, actually. And I really do love milkweed. It was just my fear speaking and besides, you've done a good job with the place. I like how the sun dances through the many holes, brightening up the darkness." Jenna still didn't think it was that great but she didn't want to cause an upset. Especially with Kirby. She might make him cry again, so she hoped the compliments worked.

Yes, he was smiling. Grinning actually.

"Oh, come on, Shelly. You know as well as I do Miss Jenna is right. This particular room is a bit drab."

"Yeah, I guess," said Shelly.

"Maybe Miss Jenna can help us make it nicer."

"Well, maybe," said a grudging Shelly.

Jenna liked the fact he called her Miss. Showed some respect and maybe emphasized the fact he really wasn't going to cause her any harm.

"Are you hungry?" he asked.

"A bit."

"I have lots of milkweed leaves I can share with you."

"Leaves? Sorry, I don't eat leaves. Any pizza? Peanut butter and jelly sandwiches? A burger? Fries?" How sad that her favorite food groups were the ones she could make fast, buy fast and eat on the run, not having time nor making the time to cook up healthy meals.

"What does she mean?" asked Kirby, looking over at Shelly again.

"No clue. Sorry, little lady, we only have leaves."

"Well, then, no thanks. I'm okay."

"Kirby, we really can't wait much longer."

Jenna stared in amazement, as Shelly tapped all sixteen legs impatiently. It was like a drumbeat, loud and clear.

"We have to tell the king and queen," she continued. "They'll want to know there's an intruder here."

A king? A queen?

"All right. Do you want me to go get them?"

"No, I will. Jenna feels safer with you. After all, she followed you. It's better if you stay with her."

She took off fast. Guess when you have lots of legs, you can move at a high speed.

"Once again, I did *not* follow you," said an indignant Jenna, masking another bout of sudden onset fear at meeting their royalty. "I have no idea how I ended up in this crazy land."

Royalty?

This was just plain nuts.

"Crazy land?"

Jenna regretted her words again. My goodness, she was going to have to really watch it, especially when she saw how hurt Kirby seemed. Why his lower lip was trembling and another tear surfaced.

Get it together.

"Oh, sorry. I've insulted your home again and I don't mean to. But the part about not knowing how I arrived here is true."

"Well, I feel the same. I have no clue how you got here either. I never noticed you behind me."

"That's because I wasn't. And hey, do you really have a king and queen?"

"Yes, we do," said Kirby. "They are in charge of our little kingdom here."

Jenna looked around. "So you call this a kingdom?"

"Yes." He smiled. "Don't act so surprised. I know you find it dowdy but it's our whole world."

"But what is all that noise? It's a constant drone."

"Oh, just us working away, gathering leaves, cleaning and lots of other stuff."

"So other caterpillars live here too?"

"Yes, many."

"Well, speaking of noise. What's that new sound? It's like a stampede of people charging around and chatting away."

Kirby smiled. "Just watch."

All of a sudden, the place came alive as at least twenty more caterpillars came pouring through the doorway.

"The king and queen are coming! The king and queen are coming!" they shrieked.

The giant insects were startled at seeing a lady in their midst, judging by how quickly they all came to a halt, their mouths opened in shock.

"It's all okay," said Kirby, addressing the new group. "I'll explain later."

They all nodded, seemed to relax and positioned themselves around the room.

"What's going on now?" asked Jenna.

"Oh, everyone loves the king and queen," said Kirby. "They get excited whenever they show up. You'll see. You'll like them, too."

Shelly raced in. "They're almost here," she exclaimed proudly. "Our king and queen."

Jenna ran to the farthest wall and sank to her knees.

Were they big? Bigger than Kirby and Shelly? Like the largest caterpillars ever?

Most of all, would they hurt her?

Two

Jenna's eyes were glued to the doorway, waiting for the first sign of the so-called royalty. She grew increasingly agitated by the moment.

It struck her again how absurd all this was. No way could it be real, so the only answer was it really did have to be a dream. A very detailed one with giant sized creatures but definitely a fantasy and a crazy one, bone-chillingly unnerving by the minute.

She was scared.

Wake up. Wake up. Dear God, please let me wake up.

Usually when she had awful dreams, she woke up fast. Frightened, but at least able to calm herself. Hopefully this one would end soon. Really, really soon.

Would they hurt her?

Hopefully not. Hopefully she could defend herself if need be.

Come to think of it, though, she couldn't help but be a little curious.

Especially now that she noticed all the caterpillars had blissful expressions on their faces, anticipating the arrival of their leaders. Maybe it would be exciting to stay asleep a while longer to meet the king and queen or at least catch a glimpse of them.

Maybe they were something special. A spectacle even.

Her mind went wild, conjuring up possibilities.

Red caterpillars or orange ones. Pink? Teeny tiny ones that lit up?

Neon green? Glowing in the dark?

There was noise.

More noise.

Like the explosive rustle of a sudden gust of wind.

Yikes!

Hey, God. Forget what I just said. Please let me sleep through this.

No such luck. Her eyes were wide open. Apparently, she was awake. Possibly still in a dream sequence but not asleep. Sleep walking. Maybe? It was all so confusing.

Oh, oh.

She realized the racket was not coming from the doorway, but from a round hole at the top of the manor.

She raised her head. Whatever was up there was drawing nearer, increasingly louder, like the roar of thunder.

She held her breath, then pushed it out in a loud gush, as skinny black legs appeared, then slowly, ever so slowly, wings, gently fluttering, lowered to the floor.

The two newcomers turned to face her.

Her eyes grew wider as she raised her head to see their faces, not sure what they were.

Hey!

Two butterflies?

With shimmery ornate golden crowns on their heads?

Really?

Oh, c'mon, this was getting outlandish. Pushing the edges of reality big-time.

But for a dream, not so bad.

Pretty creative, at least.

Where had she developed such an overactive imagination?

Sure she had always loved butterflies, but to see them wearing crowns? And huge?

Preposterous.

However, it sure beat those crazy, stress-filled dreams she was used to having. The nightmares where she ran endlessly, as if on a treadmill, but never got anywhere. The scenes that mimicked her real life.

She was glad she had stayed asleep in her dreamworld. Or at least that was what she figured was happening. Blind to the real world yet fully alert in her fantasy. She was scared but intrigued at the same time, watching the new arrivals, taking it all in.

The more she stared, the more she got used to the crowns, the more she was stunned by their beauty.

Large shiny orange and black wings spanned across the room and black trim speckled with white spots resided along the edges of their wings, as well as covering their bodies. Long antennae, coupled with those skinny, shiny black legs, completed the whole magnificent majestic picture.

She recognized them.

They really were royal.

They were monarch butterflies.

She had indeed studied them in school and had seen them flying around many times, some even landing on her hands and shoulders over the years, always flying away fast. This was the closest she'd been to one in a long time. Two of them. Huge ones. They were both gorgeous and intimidating at the same time.

They were also watching her, smiling.

Another revelation. Butterflies could smile.

Then again, if caterpillars could talk, guess butterflies could smile. At least in this world, her apparent make-believe land.

As they continued to check her out, she tried to make herself smaller. She figured she could duck and scoot under their legs and make a run for it if need be.

Or wake up.

"Who have we here?" asked the smaller of the two.

Of course, they could talk. The queen, maybe?

"Come here, little lady," said the bigger one.

Jenna stood and walked over, slow motion style, stalling. She figured she'd better obey, or else who knew what they might do. Or say.

"Don't be afraid," said the smaller one. "I'm the queen and this here is the king."

Should she curtsy? Yeah, maybe she'd better. It was the habit where she came from, as a sign of respect.

She jumped up, took hold of the edges of her skirt, and curtsied in the most dignified manner she could muster up. Duchess Kate would be proud.

"What's she doing?" asked Kirby.

"I believe it's a curtsy," said the king. "A sign of reverence."

"Very nice," said the queen. "But you don't have to do that here."

"Oh, okay. Um, are you in charge of Milkweed Manor?" Jenna asked. Just saying that made her giggle with the absurdity of it all. The type of unleashed laughing especially when you shouldn't.

Get a grip.

Giggling was not a good thing to do at the moment. Who knew? Maybe butterflies could cry, and she certainly didn't want to see that. Kirby was enough. But again, she was being rude. How could she be so obnoxious? She'd spent a lifetime always making sure others were taken care of and watching what she said so as not to offend. And here she was being an awful person who was outspoken and blunt and laughing right in their faces. The very kind of people she disliked.

Again.

For the second time.

Pull yourself together, girl.

She managed to get control of her laughter and tried to plant a serious expression on her face.

"Yes," said the queen. "I preside over Milkweed Manor, along with the king. And how did you end up here, Jenna?"

So Shelly had told the queen her name.

Jenna also noted, that although the queen's eyebrows had raised, she never made mention of her laughter. Or her rudeness. Good. She certainly didn't want to have to explain what that was all about.

"I...I don't know. One minute I was watching a caterpillar carrying a leaf, the next I opened my eyes and here I am."

"That was me," said Kirby, puffing up with pride. "I was bringing home an unusually large leaf for dinner. I saw this lady there, but she was big. Just can't figure out how she got so little and landed here."

"I don't know either," said Jenna.

"Sometimes things just can't be explained," said the queen, with a mysterious smile. "They are simply the way they are meant to be. The path our journeys lead us on."

She didn't seem in the least surprised to find Jenna there. Almost as if one day she fully expected her to join them in their community. As if she had anticipated it.

They locked eyes.

Jenna was blown away by the depth of compassion she saw there, instantly warmed by the serenity that radiated out of the queen's eyes, which managed to calm her right down.

She remembered in her grade twelve religion class, there was a large picture of a really handsome Jesus. She used to call him the 'Surfboard Jesus' for he had a dark tan, brown hair with golden streaks, looking like he was out in the sun a lot. Most memorable were his glowing eyes that somehow managed to mesmerize her, even with a quick glance at the painting.

The queen's eyes reminded her of that picture of Jesus.

Sheesh. What was happening to her here?

She seemed to flip from total fear to joy in minutes.

And God?

Here she hadn't thought of God in years and now He seemed to be on her mind a lot. What was *that* all about?

"Well, young lady," barked out the king, jarring her out of her confused thoughts. "Are you some kind of spy?"

The king was not so soothing to deal with. He seemed suspicious and not open to her being around. Couldn't say she blamed him, though. After all, she was the intruder here.

She pulled her eyes away from the queen to look at him.

"No, sir," she said firmly.

"Are you here to hurt us?" he asked. "Cause problems?"

Had to admit, she admired his bluntness. It was as if the butterflies were playing 'good cop, bad cop', trying to trip her up.

"No, sir. In fact, I am afraid you might hurt *me*."

"We would never do that," said the queen. "We are very gentle, loving, compassionate insects."

Once again, Jenna felt an overwhelming sense of peace envelop her.

For some odd reason, this beautiful queen butterfly, once again, calmed her instantly.

So they were very loving?

Good to know.

Just hoped she was telling the truth.

Otherwise...could she take down a mean butterfly with a karate chop? How many knees did they have?

On the other hand, she hoped she never really found out.

"Well, I think it's time you go home now," said the king. "Run along, little lady."

Grudgingly, she had to admit again that she admired his protectiveness. He was taking care of matters, concerned for his charges. She'd had those same feelings especially when her children were small and vulnerable. She'd do anything to care for them.

But home?

A shot of nausea hit her hard.

She almost gagged.

Probably would have, but she managed to stop herself from displaying such weakness in front of these creatures. Who knew what they'd do if they saw this? Use it to their advantage? Whatever that was?

She was also surprised at how ill she felt hearing the word *home*.

Did she even want to go back?

Now that she seemed over her fear, or most of it at least, calmed by the peace radiating from the queen, she was enjoying it here. Well maybe not thoroughly loving it, but at least intrigued. Once again it was a distraction from her life of endless problems. And hey, if this was a dream, she would wake up at some point anyway, so why not savor it all while it lasted. At least it was better than dealing with being fired, an overly busy husband, children and endless bunches of stress. No way did she want to go there at the moment. She'd been hiding out on the deck, so maybe now she could hang around here until the last second before she woke up. This was a nice break from routine, fantasy or not.

"I don't wish to go home," she said loudly and firmly, hoping to avoid all discussions and /or arguments.

"Well, you must," said the king. "You are not a caterpillar and as you can see, they are the ones who live here. The only exceptions are the queen and me."

"Well, I can learn to be like one. I can crawl instead of walk; I can learn to eat leaves. I can even help gather them."

"But why don't you want to go home, dear?" asked the queen.

Jenna was touched anew by the empathy radiating from her eyes. Her two sets of eyes, that is. She remembered reading how butterflies have simple and compound ones. Weird, but interesting. And at the moment, all were looking at her.

Wow!

This queen had quite a gift.

To be able to instantly put someone in relaxation mode was incredible.

She wanted more.

"I just don't want to, Madam Queen. I'd rather not explain, at least at the moment. Please, please, may I stay here? Please?"

Jenna held her breath as the king gazed at his queen.

She hoped they didn't try to force her life story. No way would she confide in a bunch of insects. Dream or not, that was ridiculous. Funny actually.

Silence.

Finally, the king flapped his wings twice, maybe in irritation? Or confusion? He didn't seem mad or anything. Was this a form of their intimate communication? Was he going to allow it?

The queen finally glanced away and held Jenna's gaze again.

Her heart quickened as she sucked in a deep breath and crossed her fingers.

"Yes, you may stay. At least until we figure out what is bothering you."

Jenna's breath blew out in a loud gush of relief.

Whew! No being pushed to share either.

She also had an instinctive feeling the queen wanted her here. The king too, but he was being more careful. Possibly?

Nevertheless, she was thrilled.

Surprisingly, Kirby clapped his delight and she was touched by his gesture of joy.

Tears sprang.

Drops of gratitude.

Even though Jenna still thought the whole thing a bit odd, okay, a whole lot odd, it was better than the alternative.

This was a nice respite from being a newly fired superwoman and she was determined to make the best of her adventure.

Maybe this would be the greatest vacation she'd had in ages.

If only in her mind.

Time would tell.

Three

"Yayyyy, I'm so happy you're staying," screeched Kirby.

Startled, Jenna jumped and turned around.

She had been intently watching the king and queen fly up and out the hole they'd arrived in and hadn't noticed Kirby approaching. He had a grin stretched across his face and all his eyes were twinkling like shiny Christmas tree ornaments. She was delighted at his apparent joy and acceptance, but puzzled as well.

"Well, I'm happy you're happy," she said. "But you don't know me. Why are you so glad the queen gave me permission to be here?"

"Well, when I saw you on that deck, sure you were nice to me, but you seemed so sad. Very troubled. I think being here might help you and be just what you need to make you smile again."

"You do?"

Funny, she'd been thinking the same thing. It was a really weird place to visit, and no doubt conjured up by her heart's love of caterpillars and butterflies, but for some reason she still felt compelled to stay. Irresistibly so. She felt incredibly drawn to the queen's compassion which flowed out of her, finding it soothing to her troubled soul. She even liked the king's protectiveness, for it showed he really cared for those he loved. Not to mention, everyone seemed so peaceful and happy here. After hitting rock bottom, or at least feeling like she had, she'd love to know their secret.

In short, they had something she wanted and she had to know how to get it.

"Yes," said Kirby, pulling her out of her brief respite. "You'll like it here. No one is sad for long. Oh, we go through rough times, challenging times, intense discernment, lots of changes too, but we support one another, and the king and queen guide us to be the best we can be."

"Really? The best you can be?"

"Yes."

"Please tell me. How?" Most of her life she felt she'd been just surviving, getting through the day somehow, but never really living. To be the best she could be? Impossible.

"You'll see. It's hard to explain in words. You'll just have to experience it."

"Really? Will it bring me peace?"

"Yes." He smiled. "With guidance, of course. And love. Always love."

"Love?"

"Love, for sure. It's what life is all about."

"Well, I'm all for that."

Peace, yeah right.

Surely, it was unattainable in her world. She was a mess, as far away from a state of tranquility as possible.

And *always love*?

She felt she had love once in her life. Now it was all buried under a muddle of problems, thrown away, in fact, and probably lost forever.

She took a good look at Kirby.

He appeared truly happy.

Oh, how she envied him.

She longed to feel as good as he seemed to feel. He radiated a sense of stillness and serenity that she yearned for but considered unachievable. She had been down and anxious and upset for far too long. It was now all she knew and the world in which she lived, as she chased dreams that had dissolved around her. Or at least her legal ones had. The verdict was out on her marriage and parenting skills.

But oh, she wished she knew what he knew. Felt what he felt. Lived in peace like he appeared to do.

He stared back, knowingly, as if seeing right into her heart.

"You'll get there one day, Miss Jenna. Trust me."

Trust a caterpillar?

A crawly insect?

Conjured up in her mind?

She started to grin.

Just thinking that cracked her up.

It seemed so absurd.

But when you're miserable, guess you needed to grasp at anything. So trust she would try to do. She had nothing to lose.

"And now, first things first," added Kirby. "You need food. People food."

"Oh, I don't want to be a bother. Who knows? Maybe I'll learn to really like leaves. I'm sure I've swallowed quite a few as a kid. Here, let me try."

After all, this was a dream. Maybe leaves tasted like chocolate in this fantasy land. She searched the pile by the door, picked a small shiny green one and took a bite. She began to chew.

Her face turned greener than the leaf.

"Yuck." She spit it out. "How do you exist on this?"

Kirby laughed. "Hey, I love leaves, but the queen told Shelly to tell me that people do not eat them as a rule. We are going to get you some of your own food. And what she says goes. Not that she's a control freak, but I've learned she's usually right. So, come with me, I think I need your help. I have no clue what humans eat."

He started crawling out of the room, Jenna running after him.

Suddenly he stopped.

"Hop on," he said.

"What?"

"I've got sixteen legs, you have two. You'll never keep up with me. So jump on and I'll give you a ride."

"But I have a skirt on. It's not so easy."

"It's a long one so not so bad. Here…"

He bent lower to make it easier for Jenna to climb aboard.

"This is pretty cool," she said, pulling her skirt down and glancing around.

Kirby laughed. "You might not think so when you see how high we are." He crawled out the door.

"Yikes. You're right." She stared down at the ground, so far below the Manor.

"Don't worry. I'll take my time."

And he did.

Slowly, carefully, Kirby crawled down, making her feel safe and secure.

"Wheeeeeee! This is actually fun," cried Jenna, not in the least afraid. "Kind of like one of those freaky rides at the circus. I used to love going on all the scary ones."

Kirby laughed. "Just let me know if you're nervous or uncomfortable. I'll adjust."

"Okay. But I'm fine. I know I'm safe with you. This is pretty great. I feel like a kid again."

"Good to know. Sometimes we need to just let loose and play."

Kirby landed softly on the grass, stopped, and said, "Look up."

Jenna did. "Hey, there's a large egg under the leaf above us."

"Yes, soon it will be a new caterpillar."

"Well, that's pretty exciting." She studied the creamy yellow egg. "So, if I recall correctly from school, the eggs are laid under the leaves to protect them."

Sure wished she'd learned then that caterpillars and butterflies could talk back. That would have saved her the shock of finding out they really did. She would have had a whole room full of them to confer with. It would have been lovely.

Of course, she giggled, only in dreams. Weird dreams, that is.

Nevertheless, the fact they could talk was amazing to discover here at the Manor. Maybe she really was a caterpillar whisperer and her love for them shone through and made the king and queen allow her to stay. Whatever it was, she was so glad to be here and enjoying Kirby's companionship. Once again, she thought, *a lovely break from stress.*

"Correct," said Kirby, jumping once again into her silly thoughts. She really had been going off in all sorts of tangents since being there.

Pay attention. Or else you'll miss something important.

"The leaves keep the eggs safe," continued Kirby. "Now hang on and across the grass we go."

Jenna watched as he started whistling, looking around, breathing in and out, obviously enjoying the flowers and plants and stopping to close his eyes from time to time, basking in the sunshine. Once again, she envied his total pleasure in life, for it reminded her of how she once was in her younger days. Now she was always racing around, never even noticing one bit of nature and its offerings of pure glory and loveliness. What a pity. She had wasted so much time over the years.

"Grab on tighter," he said. "We're climbing again."

Jenna raised her head, recognizing her very own tree. It was the red maple right outside her house, the one she saw Kirby disappear into when she was on the deck. Now she knew exactly where his destination was. However, she didn't have much time to think about it as they headed up. She had to hang on extra tight like he said, to make sure she didn't slip off.

"Now, it's like climbing a steep hill," she said. "Similar to traveling up on a roller coaster."

"Exactly! Don't fall off." He then abruptly stopped, crawled across a branch and hopped onto the railing.

"So, we really are going to my house?"

"Correct. Figured it's not really stealing if we take food from here. It would be considered your food too."

"Guess so." But judging by the shot of fear that suddenly engulfed her, she wasn't too crazy about being home.

She began to panic.

"Hey, this isn't some kind of plot, is it? You're not planning on just leaving me here, are you?"

Maybe it wasn't nice to think such a thing; after all he wanted her to trust him, but surprisingly Jenna was thoroughly enjoying the break from her family and wanted this dream to last forever. Or at least for a while longer. She wasn't ready to wake up yet. Maybe never. It was an awful thought, but a very real one. Sure she was being selfish, but all her energy seemed to have drained right out of her, leaving her with one fact—life was tough and she needed time away. This seemed the next best thing to running off to some other city or taking a vacation alone. Something she really would never have done before but was now a longing.

Somehow, some way, she needed to find peace. Scared as anything, she started to shake.

Kirby stopped and managed to swing his head back, so they were twelve eyes to two.

"Never," he said. "I would never do something like that. You really can trust me. Besides, the queen said you can stay."

"And what she says goes, right?"

"Right."

"Good. Is she more powerful than the king?"

"In our community, yes. But in other communities the king is the more powerful one. Sometimes they are equal."

"There are other communities like this?"

"Of course. And in each one, it is determined which monarch leads the bunch, or whether they do it together, depending on the needs of the group."

"Oh."

"I'll tell you more about it later. For now, we are on a mission."

"Okay, thanks." But she still had doubts. Lots of them. Or maybe she was just nervous being home as she immediately tensed up again. Seemed like the house created this feeling in her all the time. As far as she was concerned, it had become a place of stress, not relaxation or a tension reducer.

How had it become like this?

She remembered how excited she was when they purchased it, standing proudly behind the sold sign, arms wrapped around her husband, gazing at him with such tenderness. They'd carefully decorated each room with care and excitement and most of all, love. Once she had wanted to be able to walk in the door and feel welcomed and warm and revel in her cozy nest, a shelter from the often-crazy world outside the door.

Somehow the insane, fast-paced world she'd created had taken up residence in her head, so no matter where she was, it was always with her.

She shook her head in frustration. She just didn't know how contentment had all drifted away, mangled in a bunch of often meaningless activities. Busy work, to say the least.

Groan.

It was just so exhausting even thinking about it. How to fix it was another thing. She certainly had no answers yet. Maybe one day.

Kirby crawled across the deck and entered the living room through a tiny space in the screen door. She'd never even noticed the small hole.

She looked around. No Scott, no Ellie, no Jason. Good.

An idea formed.

"Hey, can we go into the front closet first? The one right there in the hall. Can you make it?"

"Well, I'll sure give it a try." He crawled back and forth, searching for a way to get in, then slowly squeezed through a small crack.

No wonder insects were always around. She'd never thought about it before but they somehow managed to get through anything, even the tiniest opening invisible to the human eye. In this particular situation, she was glad.

"So which shelf do you want?" asked Kirby.

"Luckily, the bottom one."

She needed to change out of this suit and had some old clothes stored there, ones she had planned to give away. They'd be too big, but she'd figure something out. She could at least take them with her, thus avoiding going to her bedroom to get her usual get-up and chance running into her husband.

Kirby slowly crawled up and landed exactly where she directed him to stop.

Jenna hopped off, looked around, burrowed under some scarfs and hats, grabbed what she wanted and stuffed it all in her pockets. Even managed to add a pair of old sneakers. Surprisingly it all fit, apparently courtesy of this magical world she was visiting. Cool.

"There. I'm ready to go now, Kirby."

"What did you get?"

"Clothes and stuff."

"Stuff?" He wrinkled his nose in confusion.

"You'll see. Later."

"Okay then, off to the kitchen we go."

"You seem to know the house well."

"I do." He smiled. "I've been here a few times."

"Really? And I've never noticed you."

"Nope, I'm good at what I do and I leave no trails."

"I see that."

"So what do you eat?" asked Kirby.

"Well, usually healthy stuff and occasionally junk food." She grinned. "Okay, who am I trying to kid, I eat a lot of unhealthy junk food, but I figure the best and easiest things to bring back are peanut butter, bread and cereal. Hmmmm...I particularly love thick chicken salad sandwiches for lunch, with tons of mayo, but that would require refrigeration. I don't suppose you have any fridges at the Manor?"

"None. But chicken? You mean those sweet, joyful birds that run around clucking?"

"Yes."

He looked horrified.

Jenna laughed. "I promise I won't bring any today."

"Good. So you have lots of pockets, right?"

"Yes. Two in my jacket and two in my skirt. The skirt ones are filled, though."

"Okay, so grab what you need. Not sure exactly what junk food is, but I'll lift you up to get it. And the other things, too. Oh, just one more point. Here's a secret. Whatever you bring to the manor, it grows in size. Or at least that's what the queen says will happen."

"Really? So, a tiny piece of bread will get bigger?"

"Correct. So even if you only bring a small amount, it will last for a long time."

"How does she know this?"

"Not sure. The king and queen know pretty much everything, though. They are very wise."

"Good to know." Guess anything goes in a dream. Pretty fantastic, really. Enchanting even. After all, she'd managed to stuff clothes in two pockets so guess if it was big, it shrinks, and vice versa. She could probably grab lots of food. Maybe even some chocolate. All rules seemed to be broken in the land of Milkweed Manor. She liked this, as she looked around for the items she wanted.

"Well, the peanut butter and cereal are up on the shelf and the bread is in that bin over there."

"No problem."

Kirby lifted her up to slide in through the door to the shelf. She was getting good at spotting entry points herself and how to get around efficiently. Jenna grabbed some plastic bags nearby that she used for school lunches, folded them to make them tiny, and started stuffing them with gobs of peanut butter, jam and cereal.

"All done here," she said, pushing it into her pockets, also adding two chocolate bars and four oatmeal cookies.

"Okay, good." He lifted her down.

"I need bread now." She scooted over to the bread bin and the two of them managed to slide it open a crack.

"Here we go." She stuffed several crusts into her pockets.

"Finished." She was rushing and knew it was because she was anxious to get out of there before she ran into anyone.

So far, so good.

Obviously, she had spoken way too soon for at that precise moment of realization, a loud voice rang out.

"Just doing my homework in the kitchen."

Darn.

Too late.

She recognized the voice.

Jenna stood still.

"What's wrong?" asked Kirby.

"It's my son, Jason. He's coming into the kitchen. Sounds like he's talking to his sister upstairs."

She watched in terror as he walked in.

Wow! She never knew he even worked at the kitchen table. Guess he took his books back to his room before she got home.

"He can't see me, right?" whispered Jenna.

"No," said Kirby. "You're too small. Remember, you never noticed me the many times I was here. But just in case, hop on and I'll crawl behind the toaster so we can hide."

"Okay, thanks."

Kirby could sure move at lightning speed when he wanted to. Guess having sixteen legs helped. We were there lickety-split.

Jenna jumped down off Kirby and peered around the edge of the toaster. She watched her son pull out a chair and spread his books, as well as his tablet, on the table. He then walked over to the fridge, poured himself a glass of milk, grabbed a plate and filled it with cookies. Whew. Close call. The cookie jar was right by the toaster. She cowered, making herself as small as possible, but he never even glanced her way.

He finally settled at the table. Like most teenagers, he loved to eat, so this was probably a favorite place of his to do work. Near food at all times. Odd, how she never knew this.

Jenna stared at him, mesmerized.

Instantly she was filled with longing as she studied his wavy blond hair, sky blue eyes, and tall lanky build.

Love filled her heart.

So did sadness.

"Your eyes are really focused on him," whispered Kirby. "It's almost like you've never seen him before."

Truth was she hadn't. Not really. Not in any deep manner. Not in a while, anyway.

"Well, I'm around him every day, obviously. But really see him? Nope, I don't. Not in a long, long time."

She'd even forgotten what he really looked like, realizing when she conjured him up in her mind, she remembered him mostly as a little toddler who worshiped her.

But he was growing up fast and the first thing she noticed was that his hair needed a trim.

How had it gotten so long and shaggy? He hated it that way.

His clothes were also a tad too small as she saw that his long sleeves didn't even reach his wrists and his jeans were up over his ankles. She hadn't noted any of this before either and she knew it wasn't the style anymore. Or a fad. Even though he liked to be independent and make his own decisions, this was not a statement. He really needed new clothes and a haircut and she had missed it all.

"How old is he?" asked Kirby.

"Twelve."

Jason's cell phone rang.

"Hello?" he said.

"Oh, okay." His eyes folded together, lines sprouted out across his forehead and he looked worried. "Our game is changed to four instead of five? And you're already there? All right, I'll find a way to get there."

"Game?" whispered Kirby.

"He plays basketball. In fact, he's a key player on the team. He loves it. Sounds like he's talking to his friend Neil. His dad is the coach so it's probably the reason why he's already there."

She noticed how Jason still seemed so anxious. Actually, tense was a mild word to describe what she was witnessing. Stressed out of his mind was more accurate. She recognized the expression. It was on her own face every time she glanced in the mirror. How sad to see her young son practically mimic her own look.

She continued to watch as he picked up his phone and started punching out numbers. She could hear it ringing and ringing. Finally, he put it down and called someone else, letting it ring and ring as well until he finally said, "Dad, what took you so long?"

He sounded frustrated. Bet he had that look on his face all the many times she had never answered him, especially during work meetings.

"Mom isn't answering her phone as usual. Can you take me to my game in an hour? The time has been changed."

Jenna gasped. The annoyed 'as usual' comment hurt. A lot. And she deserved it. She also remembered this exact same moment. It happened several weeks ago. Poor Jason had to get a ride with someone else and both she and her husband had missed the game.

Sigh.

When Jason first made the team, he had been worried about how to get to his practices and games. They lived on the outskirts of town and walking was not an option because the gymnasiums where they played were just too far away. They had promised their son that they would make sure he got there and would be in attendance at all of his games, or at least one parent would be there.

This particular incident was a no go.

Okay, granted the time had changed and they couldn't get off work, but still, it was a shame. A renege on a promise. A real failure for parenthood.

Poor Jason.

To think they were both so busy he had to stress out about getting to the games his parents had encouraged him to embrace. He shouldn't have had to worry about that. They had all agreed to support each other's endeavors. In this case talk was indeed cheap, as that old saying goes, and they had let him down.

"Okay," he said. "I'll find a ride with someone else."

She watched as he clicked off from his dad and phoned someone else.

"Hey Jarrett, I'm desperate. Can I get a ride? Okay, thanks. I sound mad? Yeah, I am. I still wanna quit. I hate playing but Mom will get mad. Dad, not so much, but Mom used to play basketball herself, was the star or something and wants me to enjoy it, too. Besides I can't bother her with my problems. She's stressed out all the time and we all promised to pitch in and help when she went back to work."

Oh, no. He knew *her* better than *she* knew her own son.

He wanted to quit basketball?

She had no idea.

"Are you crying?" whispered Kirby.

Startled, she quickly shook her head. She'd forgotten he was even there.

"Er, no."

"Yes, you are. I know tears when I see them."

"Well, what is this?" Now she was angry. "The ghost of Christmas past or something? Am I the Scrooge in this scenario? This dream sequence?"

"What do you mean?"

"Well, this situation took place weeks ago and I never even knew my own son hated basketball and that he won't talk to me about it in case he upsets me."

"No?" Now he was the one who looked startled, shocked.

"Yes. Sad, huh? But it's the truth. I didn't know any of this. It's like I don't know my son one bit."

Jenna felt destroyed. She'd been so wrapped up in making law partner she'd neglected her own family.

Part of her wanted to jump right in there and hug Jason. Tell him to stop playing basketball if he didn't want to, always answer her phone, even quit her job, just to make life easier for him.

The other part was deeply ashamed.

Incredibly traumatized.

Who didn't know their children as much as she didn't? She was a bad, bad mother, first in line to win the horrible parent award, if there was one.

The truth hit hard.

Obviously, her kids were probably better off without such a depressed, stressed-out parent. She turned to Kirby.

"Can we get out of here?"

"Are you sure?

"Yes."

"Well, okay. Guess we could sneak across the counter the other way, so your son won't see us. Quick. Jump back on."

She did, fast, imagining what her son would think if he saw his mother on the back of a caterpillar. But of course, it was her dream and she was controlling it so that would never happen. Right? And even though she was sure he would never see such a bizarre sight, she would never forget his forlorn face in this so-called fantasy. Not ever.

She wanted to scream and run away fast as once again she faced the truth—*her son was definitely better off without her.*

She needed to put distance between this horrible reality fast. She wanted time to sort it out, to figure out where she had gone so wrong.

As Kirby began the long trek back to Milkweed Manor, Jenna noticed he was moving faster. Thank goodness. The further away she got the better.

"Do you want to talk about it?" he asked, wading through the tall grass.

"Not really."

"It might be good to spill it. Sounds like you are really upset about seeing your son.

"I don't want to talk. Please don't make me."

"Okay. But I'm always here if you need me."

Had I hurt him again?

"Oh, I'm sorry. I'm being rude again, aren't I? I never used to be like this and now I seem to be doing it all the time."

"No, you're not rude. You're just really upset. Sometimes words are buried deep when we're traumatized and they take a while to come out."

"You're so kind, Kirby. So understanding and supportive. I sure don't deserve you."

"Yes, you do. Maybe now more than ever."

What did he mean by that?

She just wished she had the energy to ask.

<h1 align="center">Four</h1>

"May we come in?"

Jenna peeped out from under a pile of leaves.

She had arrived back at the Manor, enlisted Kirby to help her with a few things, decided she needed some alone time, and hid. Burrowing her head into a bunch of leaves, followed by her whole body, she believed it was where she belonged, tucked away, so she couldn't hurt anyone, and no one could hurt her.

Who was bothering her? She squinted.

Oh, wow, it was the king and queen, hovering in the doorway.

They had found her. But really, guess it wasn't too hard. This was to be her room, after all.

She really wanted to ignore them, but out of respect sat up fast, leaves spraying out everywhere.

"Oh, oh, sure. Of course, come in."

Trying hard to appear presentable, she fluffed up her hair and smoothed down her clothes, so glad she had taken the time to slip into jeans and a Tee-shirt. Funny how they fit perfectly, considering she was apparently quite a different size now. The magic of dreams. But she was much more comfortable this way, less formal and seemed to fit in better. Power suits didn't belong here. She hoped she looked at least somewhat respectable.

They floated in.

The queen stopped and looked around. A smile flitted across her face.

"Butterfly curtains. Why, they are just beautiful. How did you do it?"

Jenna was thrilled she had made the queen smile.

"I brought some material back from my house. I had this pink blanket with butterflies on it that I was going to donate. Instead I figured it would look good here, brightening up the room. Kirby had some scissors and helped me cut them and hang them. Mainly I stood on his back to reach the top to get them just right."

"Well, you did a good job."

"Thank you."

She was still amazed that caterpillars had scissors, but she was learning to accept all the weird things happening in the Manor. Kirby wore a hat, Shelly a pink hairband, the king and queen had crowns. Dreams had their own rules and she was glad of it. It kept things exciting and not the least dull.

She was also pleased the queen was happy. It made her feel good. It'd been a long time since anyone had ever praised her for anything. At work it was always 'get this job done fast' and at home it was always 'go, go, go' with endless chores and driving the children around. She never got a 'good job' ever.

A pang of guilt swept through her.

She was selfish, selfish, selfish.

When had she become this person who only thought of herself? Was she really like this all along or just had too much going on lately to think of others?

First—she literally ran away from her son. Second—when had she ever even said thank you to him?

To her daughter?

Her husband?

Certainly not in a long time. They needed affirmation as much as she did. Why couldn't she give it freely? Was she so needy that life had become all about her own wants? Or chastising others?

Don't think about that now. It was a topic for another time. She had visitors and they were speaking to her.

"So, are you content here? Do you need another room?" asked the king.

"No, this is perfect. Shelly even made me a comfy little bed of leaves to sleep on as a lovely surprise. They're pretty special, that Kirby and Shelly."

"How lovely. Yes, they are the best little caterpillars around. Hard working and kind," said the king.

"Yeah, they are," said Jenna.

But she was distracted.

She noticed the queen was now furling her brow the same way she did when she had something on her mind.

Her Majesty was worried about something.

Jenna was sure of it.

Her mind spun.

Did she want her gone?

Did they know what a bad mother she was and were disgusted?

Is that why they came for a visit? To get rid of her?

"Well, I'll be off," said the king. "I have some business to do. I am happy that you are comfortable here, Jenna. Please let me know if you need anything." He flew away fast.

Was he leaving the queen to do the dirty work?

Jenna noted she was now flying back and forth across the room. The butterfly version of pacing, perhaps?

"Is something wrong, Queen? I'm not being nosy or anything, but you look concerned. So sorry if my question is disrespectful but do you have something to tell me? Ask me?"

"How observant you are, Jenna."

Observant?

Hah!

What a laugh.

She hadn't even noticed what was going on in her own family.

Observant, she was not. Selfish, yes.

"I appreciate your interest in my well-being," continued the queen, slowing down and back to hovering. "I have nothing to tell you, but I am concerned about something. Kirby came to see me because he was with you when you ran into your son. He said you were crying." The queen floated closer. "The king and I decided I would be the best one to address this with you, both of us being mothers. I was hoping you could talk to me about what happened. Considering you don't want to go home; it must be really serious. How are you feeling now?"

Jenna was surprised. She had tried to downplay her feelings with Kirby, just not ready to talk about it, and was amazed he ratted her out to the queen. She knew he cared and was grateful for that, but it had been still too raw for her to share her thoughts. Guess ratted was too harsh a word to use, since it was clear he really cared for her. But she was still surprised.

But the queen?

The queen was different.

Once again, her compassionate, loving eyes glowed bright and touched her heart. They moved her, making her want to share everything. Kirby was very empathetic as well, but the more she stared into the queen's eyes, she was mesmerized. They appeared like *inviting opened doors* that she could walk right through and find peace. The kind of peace everyone else seemed to have here. Maybe? Hopefully?

Yes, yes, yes.

She decided she finally wanted to speak the truth.

She needed to. She had to get some help.

It was obvious this butterfly really cared and who knew, maybe dream butterflies gave good advice. They talked, they worked, they were interested in everyone and, as she had noted before, they were special, even wearing crowns. It was worth the chance to unload and see what happened and what wisdom they could impart. Kirby seemed to think Milkweed Manor was a great place and totally adored the king and queen. He seemed to think this place was just what she needed. Maybe he was right. Maybe it really would help her speak the truth for a change.

So here goes.

"Um. You're not here to kick me out, are you?"

"No of course not."

Relief flowed through her. She needed to rule that out to continue.

"Well then, I can sum up my life in three words. I hate myself. I hate who I am and all the wrong choices I have made over the years. Sorry if this is too blunt."

Jenna hung her head.

"Please, don't be sorry," said the queen in a soft, soothing voice. "It's your truth. It's how you feel. Hate is a strong word, though. May I ask why?"

Jenna started to cry. She kept her head down and soon felt soft wings engulf her. They were warm and comforting. Like the best hug she'd ever received.

"Cry, my child. Get it all out," cooed the queen. "Sounds like it's been coming for a long time."

Her kindness was Jenna's undoing. She didn't preach, didn't tell her to 'get over it,' or 'don't worry.'

Jenna especially hated when people said, "Don't worry." What did they expect her to say? "Oh, okay, I'll just stop." As if anyone could stop worrying in an instant and besides, if she was worried, there was a reason.

The queen just stayed put, allowing her to be exactly who she was.

And cry she did.

Pretty much nonstop. Big, huge wails.

Minutes ticked by.

Finally, she raised her head.

"I had no idea my son was having problems. How about that? I could be the poster parent for the worst one in the world."

The queen pulled back and locked eyes with Jenna.

"If you'd like, please feel free to tell me about this. What makes you think he does? What did you actually see?"

"See? Trouble is, I never see. I'm too locked up in my own world, especially since going back to work. But yesterday I witnessed a disheveled, troubled little boy, struggling with life and not telling me because he didn't want to upset me. It breaks my heart."

The queen still waited, not saying a word.

Jenna continued. "And to think I sometimes don't even answer his phone calls if I am busy at work. I used to always say 'family first' and now I have lost all my priorities. And you know, I thought Jason was happy. He seemed like a contented little boy. He has a ton of friends, does well at school and plays a lot of basketball. He never complains, ever."

Silence. Quiet.

Guess the queen knew stillness was key in allowing others to speak. *She was right*, thought Jenna. Time to continue to face the truth about herself, to pull away the layers upon layers of deceit which had become the world she lived in.

She had hit rock bottom. She had nothing else to lose.

"I had no idea he hated basketball," she said. "I had no idea he was feeling so stressed. And I'm ashamed that he can't tell me and will even do things he doesn't like, sports for example, just for me. As I mentioned, I never really saw him or even looked at him in any deep manner. I was always focused on my own problems and worries and concerns. Being a lawyer is a lot of work and often it is all I can think about. I never even once asked Jason how he was really doing. And if I did, it was done superficially. I just assumed life was so great for him. I took it for granted things were okay. Why I never even noticed his hair is too long and he needs a haircut and his clothes are too small due to growth spurts." Pause. "Sorry, Queen. Sorry for repeating myself."

"Oh, don't worry about that. Often it's the way we figure out solutions by allowing our problems to circle for a while. But hey, you had no trouble asking me if I was worried. You noticed and sensed *my* concern."

Jenna smiled.

"Because somehow I am calmer here. More clear-headed. I'm not running around doing a million chores and working long hours. I feel safe, alert and able to notice things. I worry less, feel taken care of and you are so nice and kind, you treat me with great respect. I admire you. I admire everyone here."

"Well, thank you. But I am a mother too and I have also experienced my children withholding their thoughts because they didn't want to upset me, or didn't think I cared, or was too busy to listen."

"Oh, c'mon. You mean, you were once like me?"

"Similar."

"How did you handle it? Please tell me. I'm desperate."

The queen thought for a while.

"Well, I stopped in my tracks one day, a lot like what you did. Sometime, I will talk to you about it. My life had fallen apart, and I was broken. Someone helped me and I discovered that often when we are at our lowest, it is the time of our greatest growth. We realize our old ways of living are just not working, so we open our hearts and search for something else."

"So... instead of sinking more into sadness, we change?"

"Some people call it change; I like to call it learning to listen to the real me, the authentic me I ignored for so long. I took the time to assess who I really was. I acknowledged my feelings, healed them and began to live life where I was totally in the present and living in the moment instead of lost in the past and the future, immersed in a world of fear. I started to really see myself and others by listening and growing in healing and wisdom."

"I can't imagine you ever being broken."

The queen smiled.

"I definitely was."

Silence.

Jenna was thinking.

Bits of wisdom and things she once believed in began to surface.

It was like they were buried treasure and the lid was finally removed, drawing her in. Surprisingly again, thoughts of God cut in and out of her thoughts. Not sure where they came from but she let them rise, rather than stuff them down.

"You know," she said, slowly and carefully. "I always hear and read about the stuff you are saying, like living in the present moment. I'm fully aware that wise people espouse this concept. Posters shout it out. Religious leaders proclaim it. I recall even at school being taught in religion class that Jesus said, *"Therefore I tell you, do not worry about your life, what you will eat or drink; or about your body, what you will wear."* I remember this for sure, for it was the answer to a bonus question on our final religion exam. I believe it was in the gospel according to Luke, if I remember correctly. The teacher expounded that God knows what we need and will always take care of us and that worry is a complete waste of time. But it just seems so hard to trust myself, God, others, when I am always full of fear and anxiety. I'm rarely even aware of the present moment. It's completely obscured with my mind swinging from one crisis to another, mostly lost in the past or future. I always kick myself for what I've done in the past and I worry nonstop about what's going to happen days and weeks ahead. The present moment? Forget it."

"What do you worry about?"

"I worry about bills and having enough money to give my children the life they deserve. I worry about my husband...and the kids. I worry about my job and my clients and whether I am representing them well. Hah! What job? I got fired. Now I'm worried about getting a new job. Oh, and I worry about myself, my health, and really, just about everything." She stared down at the floor. "Quite simply, I'm a mess."

Seconds ticked by.

The queen enveloped her again with her soothing butterfly wings but remained quiet. Jenna loved that she could take her time and feel her feelings without someone jumping in to fix them. This beautiful butterfly inspired her and gave her hope. But she definitely needed a guide.

"Er...um...maybe you can help me? Please?" she asked.

She snuggled closer to the queen, desperate, seeking her comfort and her wisdom.

"I long to be able to *really* see," she added. "Not be blind to my very own son who I love with all my heart. I don't want to be blind to anyone or anything anymore." She paused. "Especially to myself."

Silence.

Her words sunk in, hitting her hard.

In truth, she had been living a life of not being true to herself at all, therefore it filtered out and into everything she did. In fact, it tainted her whole world.

It had to stop.

Life had to be more than worries, running around in ruts and experiencing endless unhappiness. Right?

"Well, the good thing is that you recognize what is going on," said the queen, soft and slow. "It is always the first step. The key, so to speak. To stand back, as if you are an observer of your own life, and really see yourself first for who you are. To be aware of your thoughts, your feelings, to realize what is going on in your heart. To learn and to heal. And also, and this is very important, please don't beat yourself up. Ever. The process to becoming your authentic self must be done with love. Always love. And remember, life is continually evolving, and we are continually learning. Sounds like you are at that proverbial crossroad and you have decisions to make as to what the next step is. Taken in love, of course."

"You're right. It's how I really feel. I want to change. And you say you went through this too?"

"Yes."

"So what happens after we recognize what is going on?"

"You will see. It is different for each individual, as we strive not to lose ourselves in our worries and fears. As I mentioned, we heal what needs to be healed and set aside mistruths developed since childhood that tarnish the present moments in our lives."

"Mistruths?"

"Yes. Like thinking you are stupid when you're not, for example."

"Right. I do that." Jenna sighed. "It sounds so easy. At least the words do. It's seems mighty hard to live like this."

"Practice, dear. It takes practice. Most important, and I know I already said this, but I cannot stress this point enough...loving yourself. It is the nucleus from which all else flows."

Loving one's self.

Hah! Hard to do when you hate yourself.

Guess this was what Kirby meant when he said she needed to be here now more than ever.

She had a lot to learn.

And the queen, the king and all the caterpillars could teach her real truths. She was sure of it.

Bizarre. Sounded crazy. But it seemed to be true.

She had been so angry with herself, practically her whole life, but to be honest, it felt good to admit it all instead of trying to be superwoman.

Okay.

This was it. A moment of true reckoning.

She was on the brink and she needed to make a decision.

She was figuratively laying down her super woman cape.

It was time and she had nothing to lose.

Sure looked like she had to start with the basics though, and learn to care for herself first. It did make sense and seemed right that it really was the entry point to transforming herself. Maybe love was really all it took. Always love, as the queen and Kirby had said. But first, love for oneself. Something she'd never thought much about before, always caught up in other people's needs and taking care of them.

Jason's worried face flashed up again. As if jumping out of nowhere.

"But maybe I should go back now," she said urgently. "I think Jason needs my help."

"Are you ready to go home?"

"I don't know. I feel safe here. Sheltered, and I'm learning so much."

She thought for a minute.

Already she'd forgotten.

Start at the beginning.

"No, I really don't feel ready," she said. "I feel I need to help myself before I help anyone else. Am I right?"

"Only you can answer that, Jenna. Just take it a day at a time. You will know when you need to go back. You will know when you are ready. And I am always here to talk to you, if you need it."

"Thanks again. May I ask you another question?"

"Yes, certainly."

"Just curious. Kirby says there are many communities like this. Some the king is in charge. Some the queen. Is that true?"

"Yes, it is. I am in charge of this community, with the help of the king. We all struggle with issues involving becoming our real selves but most of my charges struggle with concerns relating to motherhood and parenting. Some communities have the king in charge for they struggle with fatherhood issues and some communities have an equal balance of king and queen."

"Really? And I ended up here because I have mother issues. And all sorts of *me* issues too."

The queen smiled. "Once again, only you can answer this."

Jenna smiled back. "Guess we both know the truth to this. A resounding yes. I'm a bad mother. But I seem to grasp that there is some hesitation in your sharing. That you are wanting me to search my own heart for answers, not depend on someone else's opinion."

"Exactly."

"But you give guidance, right?"

"I listen and share what I've learned. But only you can figure out what works for you."

"Yeah, you're right. But hey, can I help?"

"Help?"

"Yes. Do you have jobs I can do around the Manor? I'd love to get involved. To earn my keep. Also to not just wallow in my self-hatred."

The queen's eyes lit up.

"Well, I certainly don't want you wallowing in self-hatred. Let me think about it. However right now I believe you need more sleep. I can see the fatigue in your eyes. Why you can barely keep them open."

"Would that be okay? I do feel tired and just wiped right out."

"Yes, you should sleep. You need the rest. It is necessary in this journey for it can be very healing and restorative."

"Thank you."

She yawned and curled up again, sinking into the warmth of the leaves, figuring she hadn't slept for long hours all at one time in ages. Maybe never.

"Oh, one more thing." Jenna sat up. "I studied butterflies in school. Was fascinated by them, by the way. It's amazing that you talk but one thing was drilled into my head. I thought you couldn't hear. I thought you had no ears."

The queen smiled. "Well, we really do but not the traditional ones. Ours are on our wings. There we sense sounds and vibrations which allow us to hear in our own way. But I'm sure you realize by now that Milkweed Manor is an enchanted place. There are no limits here. We don't necessarily adhere to earthbound rules. We make our own. I can hear you perfectly and I can talk."

No limits.

Jenna liked the sound of that.

It gave her hope.

Her last waking thought was a feeling that the butterfly had leaned over and kissed her goodnight. A sweet gentle kiss. She couldn't help but think it was a healing one rooted in love and acceptance. That this was another step to finding peace.

She sure hoped so.

Five

Jenna's eyes popped open. She yawned, looked around, then yelped.

Where was she?

She'd been having lots of dreams lately. All about caterpillars and butterflies and loud noises. Sometimes they were scary. Sometimes soothing.

But this wasn't her bedroom.

Where were all the colorful landscape paintings spread across her walls? Her oak dresser with the oval mirror?

What the...?

Panicking, she sat up and scanned the room.

Tree? She was in a tree?

She looked down at her feet.

Leaves? She'd been sleeping on leaves?

The space was small, with a ray of sunlight peeping in through a side window. Not really a window but a hole with butterfly curtains fluttering around in a slight breeze.

Then it clicked.

Ahhhh, the butterfly curtains were the giveaway, making total sense, since she had made them.

She sighed in relief.

Right. Milkweed Manor. That was where she was.

It wasn't a dream. Or actually, it probably was. Just not a nightmare. Or at least not yet.

Whatever was going on, she was dwelling with caterpillars presided over by two butterflies.

Go figure.

It sounded so silly even saying that.

Ridiculous, actually.

She pinched herself again.

Was it really true? Ouch, guess it was. It still hurt, and she was still feeling pain in her dream, in this imaginary land. Who knew what was going on?

Her husband and kids would never believe this.

She hardly did herself.

Somehow, she had found herself living in the midst of a fantasy. What was most shocking was the fact the kindness of the butterflies and the caterpillars made her want to stay. Actually, it was even more than that. These creatures were at peace. They radiated a sense of calm and enjoyment of life. They apparently lived in the moment, which was something she aspired to do as well. Certainly, if it brought the same serenity in life that it did them.

Once again she acknowledged, that they had what she desperately wanted.

She was curious, intrigued but still tired. She yawned. Loudly. So darn tired. She had halted her mad race in life, or actually her boss had, which left her acknowledging that she was completely worn out. Endless responsibilities and endeavors smashed around and just thinking about them still exhausted her.

Plus the realization her son was unhappy.

Jason.

His tense, worried face popped into her mind. Horror suffused her as she suddenly remembered the visit yesterday. Guess she'd been blocking it out, tossing it out of her mind and heart. It was just too painful to dwell on.

She would never forget how sad he looked.

She loved her son with all her heart but it sure seemed like her brand of love just wasn't good enough. He was certainly not the happy boy she thought he was.

Panic flared.

Maybe she should go home now.

Was it time?

She took stock.

Still, a resounding no washed through her.

She just wasn't ready. Yes, she was a bad mother for not rushing back, but still something kept her here.

She yawned again.

Deep-seated fatigue, maybe? A sense of failure? Disgrace?

Or…the search for something new? Or…something she had lost?

Craving serenity?

Whatever it was, she couldn't face her son right now. She was a mess and simply no good for him. She was going to trust the queen and believe she would know when it was time to go. Or wake up. Or whatever. Her children were in safe care with her husband, until she made it back.

If ever.

Because they really were probably better off without her.

If she did head home though, she would never speak of what she saw and experienced at the Manor for fear they would think she'd gone crazy.

So not now. She couldn't leave in this frantic, cluttered state of mind.

One day. Maybe. She hoped.

But not yet.

She'd made up her mind.

Beginning today, she was going to try to work on herself.

Please, God. Please help me.

There she went again.

Praying to God.

Almost as strange as hanging with caterpillars and butterflies. However, it was her reality at the moment, so she'd go with it.

Sooooo…just for today she was going to make an attempt to love herself and live more in the present, deal with the present, really see the present for a change. She recalled recommending friends, even clients, to do this when stressed, even suggesting it to her husband from time to time for he was a real worrywart as well. Oh, who was she trying to kid. She was projecting out on Scott when in fact she was the real queen of stress. It was time she took her own advice. She would make a vow not to get wrapped up in the clutter of anxiety. Maybe with practice she could carry this way of living back to her family.

Maybe?

She was lucky on one level. She had four guides here to help her. Kirby, Shelly, and the king and queen. They were kind and sweet and wise. She really liked them. Most of all, she had a lot to learn from them.

They seemed happy.

She wasn't.

She had to know how they did it. What was their secret to peace? Was this it? Was it just acknowledging the truth about one's self? Was it just living in the present? Not being mired down with past and present worries? Was there more to it? And how do I get there? What were all the steps?

Her family could wait a bit. They'd be happier without her messing up their lives.

Right now she wanted to see her wise caterpillar friends, ridiculous as that sounded.

In fact, she couldn't wait to chat with them. To take mental notes. To learn and study.

She jumped up and first tidied her bed by shoving stray leaves back where they belonged. Guess she'd been tossing and turning all night, judging by how messy they were. Whistling, feeling light-hearted for a change, she headed out, and hearing recognizable voices, followed them.

"Good morning, Kirby, Shelly," she said, entering what looked like a kitchen, with large tables and multiple wooden platters.

"Good morning," they said, big smiles on their faces, snowy white aprons wrapped around their waists.

A caterpillar had a waist? And wore an apron?

"Oh, so this is where you took my stuff last night?"

"Sure is," said Kirby. "You were falling asleep when we got here, said you weren't hungry, so I figured you needed some rest and took you straight to your room. We hung the curtains and I left."

"Right. And I slept straight through the night."

"How are you doing now?"

"Not too bad. I had a visit from the queen."

"Oh."

Jenna detected a wave of worry flitting through his eyes. Easy to see when you're looking at twelve of them. Too bad humans didn't have more. Maybe, just maybe, she'd really *see* what was going on for a change.

She opened her mouth to say something, but he jumped in faster.

"Hope you didn't mind that I told the queen about what happened yesterday."

"Not at all," she quickly said, hoping to reassure him. "I know it's because you care."

"Yes, I do. A lot." His eyes started to twinkle. "Bet talking to the queen made you feel better."

"Sure did. She is very wise."

"Definitely."

"But thanks for being there for me yesterday, Kirby. Just couldn't talk about it yet but you helped me enormously. You didn't push and just let me be. I appreciated that."

"No problem at all. And by the way, you look beautiful. Well rested and definitely less tense."

She sure didn't feel beautiful or look it, but she didn't want to insult him by disagreeing. He was sincere and probably really meant it, in his own mind. Certainly not in reality.

"Well, thanks. I slept well. So, um, may I help you?" She noticed he had kept busy placing leaves in bowls during this whole interchange. She felt lazy just doing nothing.

"Sure," said Kirby.

"What are you doing?"

"Preparing breakfast for the gang," said Shelly, crawling over. "Here, could you please put this platter of leaves on the table? It's right through there." She pointed off to the left.

"Sure."

Carrying the large plate carefully, glad that it wasn't one of the bigger ones, she struggled to make sure nothing blew off as she entered what she figured was the dining room.

She stopped in her tracks.

It was actually quite pretty.

A huge table sat in the middle, dominating the room. Not only was it wide, but very tall as well, made of branches that had obviously been woven together. Guess the caterpillars all stood as they ate which was probably the only way they all fit in. A shiny golden chandelier was centered over it giving the effect of elegance yet managing to project coziness and warmth. A big round silver gong was off in the corner. Actually, it looked like the lid off a garbage can, and was probably used to summon everyone, for there were multiple entrances, and judging by the numerous place mats, it appeared like a lot were expected for dinner.

Oddly she wasn't afraid. Not really. Well, maybe a little?

"And here is *your* food," said Kirby, bringing in a small platter, just the right size for her.

She glanced at it. He was right, or rather the queen was right. The food certainly expanded here for there were two large sandwiches, yummy peanut butter oozing out of them and a shiny red apple lay beside them.

Her stomach grumbled with hunger at the sight of it.

"But we didn't bring back any apples."

"I know." He grinned. "I instructed the troops to bring home any fruit they find for you. I think someone spotted a banana yesterday and they were going to see if it's still there today."

Jenna was touched.

"Well, thank you."

"Here, I'll stand and you can crawl up my back to put your platter on the table."

"Great. I was wondering how I was going to do this."

She scurried up, carefully balancing the platter and was impressed again when she saw the numerous plates and bowls of leaves spread across the tabletop. Definitely a feast going on here.

"Would you like to ring the bell?" asked Shelly, entering with a large container, which she placed on the table as well.

"Oh, sure. I saw the gong there and figured that was what you used to get everyone's attention."

"Yes. It's how we let them know that breakfast is ready. Otherwise they'd be so engrossed in their work, they'd forget."

"Forget? I don't think I've ever forgotten a meal. And I have the fat to prove it." She glanced down at her ample curves and once again was struck by how she had way too many of them. She grimaced. She had struggled with her weight all her life. Up thirty, down ten, up forty and so the craziness continued. She just couldn't seem to stick to a diet and all her effort never really amounted to anything. It was like pounds were glued to her, refusing to melt away.

"Stop," said Kirby.

Whoa! He sounded harsh.

"Pardon?" Jenna glanced up, startled.

"Please, don't cut yourself down. Ever," scolded Kirby. "We don't do that here."

"Er... I was just joking."

"No, you weren't."

He was right.

She wasn't.

She often made cracks about her fat but the fact was, she was overweight and bothered by it. But stress eating had become a way of life for her. She even hated to admit that she ate donuts by the boxful and had packages of cookies in her bottom drawer at work and in her night stand at home. No way would she confess that to anyone. It was her own dirty little secret. She was sure her husband didn't even know.

She noticed Kirby continuing to stare at her, challenging her.

"Yeah, I wasn't," she answered, embarrassed. "But hey, enough of me. I'd love to ring the bell." Hopefully this would end this uncomfortable conversation.

Uneasy and refusing to look at him, she crawled down his back fast.

"Well, I'm ready, Shelly, to go bang that gong."

"Follow me."

"I'm right behind you."

When they arrived, Shelly turned around and stared knowingly. She said softly, "Kirby's right, you know."

"About what?"

Jenna decided to play dumb, not exactly sure what the caterpillar was referring to. But of course, she really did know.

"It is never nice to criticize yourself, to knock yourself down, to dislike any part of you. You need to love, accept and take care of yourself. Sure change can happen, but it comes out of love, not hate."

She simply didn't know what to say. Like everyone else, Shelly spoke the truth, but really...love herself?

Love? Oh, c'mon.

Hard to do, when there was so much about her body to hate. Not to mention how tight her jeans felt around her waist.

Then again, she had promised herself that she would at least make an effort to care and stop the tormenting round of insults she hurled at herself each day. She had always been convinced she was the fattest person ever, larger than an elephant even, and constantly looked awful. At least in her mind. Or, that was what Scott always said. He used to tell her she looked beautiful every day. Just like Kirby.

Sigh.

She wished she'd had those days back with her husband. Days of loving each other and being vocal about it.

Oops.

Shelly was staring at her, obviously waiting for a response.

"Well, you're definitely right, Shelly. You and Kirby have pointed out something I do often, cut myself up. I know it's wrong, I see that so clearly now. I'll try not to do that anymore but it's so hard to break old habits."

"Good. But relax. It all takes time and practice. Now here, hop up," said Shelly. "We have a job to do."

Fortunately, she was saved from any further discussion. She was still not up to it, she thought as she climbed up on Shelly's back and was raised up to hit the bell with a gavel. Life was on a constant spin at the moment and she was reeling from it all. And right now, her ultimate goal was just to hit that gong.

In fact, to create the necessary noise, she was using a large spoon, since the gavel was way too heavy for her to lift.

She threw her whole body into it, as she banged it twice, startled at how loud the sound was but guessed it was necessary, especially to be heard over the constant noise that seemed to surround Milkweed Manor. This was without a doubt an ear-splitting place in general. Odd, but true. Sometimes she had to put her hands over her ears to block out the noise. It didn't seem to bother anyone else though. Guess her ears were more tender or they were just used to it.

Shelly quickly took her back and dropped her off near Kirby.

"Thanks. That was cool."

"No problem," said Shelly. "I'll be right back. I just need to grab another plate from the kitchen."

Suddenly, Jenna felt the floor shake.

She watched in awe as a stampede of caterpillars charged into the dining hall through every possible opening. It was stunning to watch. There were hundreds of them and as they piled in, she felt swarmed, and it was beginning to be a bit scary. She started to tremble.

"Are you okay?" asked Kirby.

"Well, they're all so big and there's so many of them. Will they hurt me?"

"Nah, don't worry, I'll take care of you. They won't hurt you. We are all very gentle. Here, I'll stand right behind you if that will make you feel better."

It did and she was glad of the support.

"But why do they all look so different? And why are there pockets of stuff on the floor? Looks a bit like thin paper. And why do they stop and eat it? Kinda gross, don't you think? Can't they wait a few more seconds to eat the leaves at the table?"

"Oh." He started to laugh. "Don't you know? As we grow, caterpillars shed their skin five times. We molt. Sorry, I should have mentioned this before. This is something you'll see quite often here. Some are in the process right now. And yes, they do eat it. It's our tradition and also full of rich healthy vitamins. It's bonus food for us."

"Oh. That makes sense now. I do remember reading about such a thing, but actually seeing it is quite different. Sure wish I could shed my own skin. Not sure I'd want to eat it, though, but I love the whole concept of out with the old and in with the new."

Kirby laughed. "Well, maybe you can shed. Figuratively speaking, that is."

Not a bad idea at all, but she still was well aware of all the doubts that flooded her, truly not believing that peace and love could come her way.

Keep trying, she said to herself.

She had nothing to lose and maybe saying this to herself every day, even every minute, might help. Hopefully, in the midst of her brokenness, a tiny sprout of hope just might grow. Maybe?

She crossed her fingers, longing for something she didn't have. At least yet. Maybe never.

"Come on, we're about to eat," said Kirby, jumping into her thoughts.

He helped her up onto a tall stool so she would be even with the table.

"Did you put this chair here for me?"

"Yes, I did." He smiled. "You are way too small for the table."

"And you actually made it?"

"Yes. Wove it together from sticks I collected."

"Did you make the table too?"

"Yes. With help, of course."

"You're very sweet and also incredibly handy. Thank you for looking out for me."

"Any time," he said. "That's what we do here. We help each other."

Jenna felt all warm inside. Toasty, even. It felt wonderful having someone watching her back and looking out for her. It sure seemed like she had the best friend ever in Kirby. She was pretty darn lucky. She grinned. Okay, it was kind of weird to have a caterpillar for a best friend, but hey, if it worked, it worked.

"Attention, everyone," said Shelly, crawling back into the room. "Some of you have already met her, but for those who haven't, this is our guest, Jenna."

A loud murmur arose as they greeted her with nods, smiles and warm eyes. Lots of warm eyes. So many eyes it began to freak her out. She felt Kirby slide closer, smiling at her, offering support again, helping her calm down.

And then it hit her.

This was one of the qualities she was missing.

The ability to really see another's pain, hurt or fear, like Kirby did. He easily sensed how nervous she was and took action to comfort. She was usually so caught up in worries and problems that she saw nothing but a reflection of her own stress. She had totally missed her son's pain. Kirby would have seen it in a flash.

As she had told the queen that very morning, the fact she was really blind to others had to stop.

It hit her again that she really did have much to learn here.

And the knowledge that this group of caterpillars and butterflies also welcomed her immediately was incredibly amazing. She had sure lucked out in this breathtaking land of dreams.

Remember your manners.

"Hello, everyone. Thank you for letting me stay here," she said.

They continued to smile back. Automatically, she instantly picked up a sandwich. She was still nervous and, being a stress eater, she wanted to stuff her feelings of anxiety away.

"Not yet," whispered Kirby, nudging her.

"Sorry."

She dropped the sandwich and literally sat on her hands.

Another rustle and the sound of flapping.

"Attention everyone," said Shelly. "The king and queen have arrived."

They flew in, magnificent and regal, each one taking up the end spot. Of course, they would be here. They were the head of this little kingdom. How could she have forgotten?

"Hello, everyone," said the king. "It's a brand-new day and time to start anew."

Start anew.

Beautiful words to live by, thought Jenna. Sure wished she could.

Lots of good mornings rang out, so she joined in. Somehow seeing these beautiful butterflies always made her feel good. Almost content.

"Now let us thank God," said the queen. "Or whoever or whatever you choose to embrace, a higher power, another deity, nature, and so on. Please always remember, it is your own individual choice and we all respect everyone's decisions here."

To Jenna, it was God, but she truly did value everyone else's choices. Many were raised in a certain faith, others chose their own beliefs and no one had the right to judge. She was pleased to see this community felt the same and strived to exist in harmony. It was truly beautiful and heartwarming. Very ecumenical. Amazing how progressive they all were.

But, hey, who would have figured caterpillars, led by butterflies, prayed?

They didn't use her excuse, *Oh, I'm too busy.*

More and more, this was definitely a world she wanted to belong to, to emulate, without a doubt, and she felt lucky to be here.

If only in her dreams.

Silence rang out.

"We give thanks for this food, for friendship, peace and love, always love," said the king, short but succinct.

"Amen," said the caterpillars.

Jenna looked around at the serene expressions on all the faces and instantly relaxed.

Life was good. At least for the moment.

"Now we begin," said Kirby.

And peanut butter had never tasted so amazing, not to mention the juicy apple. It was enriched by the happy atmosphere around the table. No wonder her food at home often tasted like cardboard. It lacked the secret ingredients: love, support, joy and kindness.

She scanned the room again, enjoying the excited conversations drifting around her. Mostly it seemed to be about each one's different stages of growth. There was much laughter and encouragement and support. No cell phones. No upsetting each other. No loud voices. No one figuring out who had to drive someone somewhere. Everyone just intent on listening and enjoying one another and caring, really, really caring, just the way they were. No one was trying to organize anything or control or change each other.

The contrast to her own way of life was startling.

It was nothing like her table at home.

In her kitchen, everyone was distracted and still used their phones. She was the worst offender and always said it was because she couldn't miss a call from work, but really, maybe she was just using that as an excuse to not pay attention, to not know what was going on. Knowing might mean caring, listening, possibly even having to take some form of action, and she had no time for that. Or so she thought. She seemed to have chosen to live in a world of chaos and it had oddly become her bizarre safety net. But in so doing, she had missed the pain on her own son's face. What was once her comfort zone had huge holes in it and she'd fallen right through.

How horrific.

Once again, she figured she was a bad, bad mother.

But was peace really sustainable?

Could it be forever?

Could she live like the caterpillars and their royalty?

"Is it always like this?" she asked Kirby.

"Like what?" He looked puzzled.

"Oh. Lots of conversations and really supporting and caring for one another."

"Yes, of course it is. The king and queen have rules. Eating times are for community sharing and building up each other. We support one another at all times."

"It's a great idea. The way meals really should be eaten and shared." And one she should know already. She sure had gone way off kilter and knew she definitely should implement these rules when she got home. She knew some families did. She just never bothered or got around to it. Or to be honest, never wanted to do it. It was like being at the base of a mountain and trying to climb up. It seemed so foreboding so why try?

But here it worked.

She had witnessed it firsthand, even in dream form.

And she wanted it.

Badly.

Oops. Something was happening.

Her heart beat fast when the queen floated over to hover above her.

Jenna bathed in her smile and aura of serenity.

"Did you really mean it when you said you wanted to help out, Jenna?" she asked.

"Yes, of course."

"Well then, please, come with me. I have an important job for you.

Six

I wonder what they have in mind?

Nervous but excited, Jenna followed the king and queen down a hallway. She thoroughly enjoyed watching how elegantly they floated. Why, they never walked, despite having those long black legs. It was like a comment on how they lived their lives—soaring, flying, with grace, beauty and treasuring every moment. She admired them so much and sure wished she could float too. Metaphorically speaking, that is, since she didn't have wings. It looked so tranquil. So enticing. So freeing.

But a special job?

Sounded a bit ominous.

It reminded her of all the so-called special jobs her boss had given her, challenging her, expecting perfection, hanging the possibility of a partnership over her head. Immediately, her nerves accelerated as she acknowledged her fear that she wouldn't be able to do a good enough job or measure up. She never seemed to succeed at work or at home, for that matter. She hoped this one was easy. She'd hate to let down the king and queen and be forced to leave the Manor in disgrace.

Which might induce her to wake up, which she didn't want to do yet. Especially now she was loving it here.

The butterflies hovered at an entry way, turned and flew in. Jenna followed at a run.

"Wow."

Stopping in her tracks, she looked around.

She was standing in a large space, dimly lit by a hole in the top right-hand corner that let in a limited amount of sunshine. It was rather spooky, with what looked like bags hanging from the ceiling, strung across the room. She couldn't make out what they were, for they were all high up, occasionally swaying back and forth. Very eerie-like.

She suddenly felt afraid. Her imagination flew wild.

Was this some kind of dungeon or something?

Were the *bag-things* the remnants of other people who had somehow invaded Milkweed Manor and failed?

Were they planning on leaving her here?

Or were they just trying to scare her?

To tell her she would end up hanging if she didn't do things their way?

Were they mean, after all? Cruel?

Glancing over, she noticed the king and queen were floating in place, as if treading water, watching her carefully. They always seemed so kind. Surely, they would keep her safe, right? Surely this was some kind of good thing, right?

Swallowing her fear in one loud gulp, she made a split decision to trust them and check out the room in a more methodical manner. After all, they'd shown her nothing but gentleness so far. Curious, she had to know what was going on there.

Slowly, she walked around, scanning the area, trying to study the objects to figure out what they were. As her eyes adjusted to the darkness, she could make out branches secured across the ceiling. The bag things, for she still wasn't sure what they were, appeared to hang off them.

Wait a second.

Oh my goodness.

She knew what they were.

Her heart raced. Excited, she turned to face the king and queen.

"They're chrysalises? That's the correct term, right? If I remember from my biology classes, they are all going to be butterflies like you, aren't they?"

"Yes," said the queen. "You are correct. Our royal duties are to supervise the caterpillars throughout all their many stages of growth, until they transform themselves into butterflies. We guide them, love them, and make sure they make it."

"But this is beautiful." A bit creepy too, but she didn't want to say that in case she hurt their feelings.

"Yes, it is." The queen smiled. "Don't be afraid, nothing will harm you here."

Jenna was surprised the queen saw through her fake façade, since she was trying to hide the apprehension she felt. She didn't have as much as when she first entered, and her excitement was real, but she still held on to some fear. But then again, she shouldn't be surprised. The queen was very astute, had super powers of observation and seemed to see it all. Once again she longed to be like that one day. It was a skill she needed to develop, first by calming her constantly wildly racing mind to begin to really *see*.

"And your job," continued the queen. "That is, if you would like to help us, is to supervise this room. The chrysalises are watched around the clock."

She pointed to a caterpillar off to the side who waved. Jenna hadn't even noticed him in the dim lighting.

"Really? The chance to see a butterfly hatch? Metamorphosize? A dream since a kid. I'd love to help. It would be a complete honor. But what if I mess up?"

There I go again. Always the downer. I had absolutely no faith in any of my abilities. Another pattern since a kid, deeply ingrained, seemingly forever.

"You won't," said the king. "We have total faith in you. And if it will make you feel better, it won't just be up to you. We have other people helping, too."

"But what do I do?"

"You watch," said the queen. "You observe. You fix chrysalises that are falling over and may need some help. You guide butterflies who are trying to emerge and get tangled up and need some assistance."

Observe?

That was almost laughable since, as she had noted before, skilled observational powers were something Jenna lacked. But she was touched by the trust this royal pair seemed to place in her. Also thrilled.

"I'll certainly do my best."

"Yes, I know you will. And you'll see many emerge, I hope. They are all at various stages of their development and mostly handle matters themselves. It is only occasionally that we step in to assist." The king pointed to a small chair. "Here is a place for you to sit, if you'd like. Kirby made this for your room, but we figured it would give you a place of comfort while you take up your post here, providing you want to. So, it's a yes?"

"Yes. Definitely."

She ran over and perched on the chair.

"How kind of him. It's just perfect." She grinned. "I'm ready."

"Good. We thought you might enjoy this. Oh, by the way, Kirby is making another one for your room as well. Thank you for agreeing to do this," said the king. "This will allow one more caterpillar to hunt for food. It takes a lot to feed this tribe."

Jenna could feel her eyes grow wider and somehow she knew they were shining, as she basked in their approval.

"Here, my dear. You might need this." The queen took something off the wall, a thin metal item that was hanging there, and handed it to her. "It's a small tweezer. Just in case. This might help the butterfly if he or she is trapped or needs a hand. But as the king said, mostly there will be no problems and it will be a natural birth."

"Oh, okay."

"There are also stepladders over there in various sizes." The queen pointed to the other side of the room. "You may need them to reach the chrysalis."

"Great."

"Any questions?" asked the queen. "Are you feeling okay about it now?"

Jenna took note of her feelings, which was a rarity, for she mostly spent time avoiding them.

"Yes, I'm good now, thanks."

And she really was.

As she watched the butterflies leave, along with the caterpillar, she sure hoped nothing bad happened. She wasn't sure she was capable of saving the day, so to speak. But she really was glad to be helping, nervous or not. It was like earning her keep for the fact they were allowing her to stay there, something she was very grateful for. It made her dream-world more peaceable.

So, now, first things first.

She got comfy and settled down to watch.

The minutes ticked by.

Silence overtook her.

Somehow this room seemed immune from all noise, chatter and even all those loud beeps she heard everywhere else. It was almost unnerving. Her whole life had been filled with commotion which barely gave her even a moment to think.

Now, she had all the time to think.

And she wasn't sure she liked it.

All sorts of tangled thoughts emerged. All making her feel awful, underscoring the fact she was a failure.

A chrysalis moved. Oh, good. Whew. A diversion.

She jumped up, grabbed a ladder, climbed up and inspected it. All seemed fine. So next she decided to inspect each chrysalis. Her eyes, increasingly adjusting to the lack of light, noted that some of them looked close to popping open and she could actually make out the butterfly nestled inside. It was breathtaking. A true miracle of nature, one she hoped to witness.

"Let me know if any of you need help," she said out loud, not sure they could hear her, but just in case. She wanted them to know she was there for them in every way.

She sat back down. It was still so quiet. Not so eerie now, she was getting used to it, even beginning to feel a bit tranquil.

Serenity. A rare commodity in her world.

Then she remembered how the queen had suggested she step back, figuratively speaking of course, and observe and pay attention to how she felt.

Let's try it.

Calm. She felt calm. Even a bit joyful at the trust the king and queen had in her.

It'd been a long time since she'd felt like that.

She'd forgotten what it was like to experience serenity, or joy, for that matter. She remembered many past moments, when she had really enjoyed life. The night her husband proposed, the first time she held each child, Christmas mornings when the kids were young and excitement was in the air. What a contrast to this past Christmas, when no one seemed to even want to be together and all they cared about was once again, their cell phones. Herself included.

How had she lost her joy in life? Especially to technology and social media and just plain busyness? How had computers and gadgets ended up controlling her and not the other way around? She'd read lots about technology and young people and how to supervise their involvement in these areas. She just never followed their advice, nor made her family do so, either.

How had happiness and contentment flitted away when once it had been so important to her to hang on to it?

Now it was all lost in overloaded schedules, craziness, fear, worry.

Fear.

She had to admit that fear seemed to be number one in her life. It had gripped her often, daily, turning everything into one big hassle.

Fear sucked the life out of everything.

She closed her eyes, summoning up a vision of the king and queen. They seemed happy, engaged in life, focused and content. She wanted to be like them so badly. She pictured their grace and beauty.

Minutes ticked by.

All of sudden, as if out of nowhere, the haze cleared.

She opened her eyes.

She understood why she was in this special room. Why she *needed* to be here.

Bet the queen had carefully chosen this as her classroom, a place to teach her how to be present, to live in the moment, to heighten her powers of observation. She simply had to, if she were to make sure the chrysalises were taken care of. It also gave her silence to think, to meditate and contemplate. All of these things she never did. Instead she would get all caught up in her anxieties and let them rule her. How interesting that by stepping back and simply observing, they seemed to have less power over her. She recognized them for what they were—thieves—stealing her away from being fully aware in the moment, and only creating anxiety and confusion.

Oh, she had so much to learn. So darn much.

The quiet there was growing on her.

She was beginning to even like it.

She began to relax.

And feel tired.

Couldn't help herself. She yawned and closed her eyes again.

Stay awake, stay awake...

"Rise and shine, little one."

Oh no.

Her eyes flew open.

She jumped up, almost stumbling into the queen.

"Oh, I'm so sorry. I fell asleep. I let you down."

She felt frantic, like a little kid, fully expecting to be yelled at for not doing her job. See, she knew she would botch it. They should have never trusted her.

But the queen just smiled.

"It's okay, dear. It is a lot to take in, the quiet, the careful watching of each chrysalis. You have taken good care of them but it is easy to succumb to sleep. Don't worry. We've been checking in on you because you are new and trust me, all of us have dozed off from time to time."

Jenna started to cry at the queen's loving kindness and compassion. Once again, she felt it'd been ages since anyone had ever treated her like that, or she had treated someone else like that.

Yikes. She really was selfish.

"I don't deserve you being so nice to me."

"Yes, you do. It is the way you should always treat yourself, as well. With gentleness. It is the way we grow, in love and support. Anger and berating yourself never works."

She was right, thought Jenna. All the rage in the world had never induced one single change in her.

"Er, Queen?"

"Yes."

"It was hard at first but later I felt fleeting moments of peace here. But you seem to be peaceful all the time. You radiate a quietness that helps me feel calm just by being in your presence. I'm trying hard to live in the present moment, or at least I want to, but I find I'm still worrying all the time and often filled with fear. It's like being in fog trying desperately to see things but feeling lost instead. It's driving me crazy."

The queen grinned.

"Remember, I was once like you."

"Yeah, right. You mentioned that. It still seems hard to believe."

"It's true."

She flew closer.

"I told you one day I'd tell you my story. Would you like to hear it now?"

"Yes, of course. I'd be honored."

"Well, I was not always so peaceful. I was once a rebel caterpillar. Mischievous, full of pranks, a real rascal."

"Really? You?"

"Yes. Despite being a mom with lots of responsibilities, I still wanted to swing through trees and bushes and take all sorts of chances. I was a daredevil, basking in tempting fate. One day, I invited my best friend Alice to join me. She was beautiful, sweet and very kind. She was afraid of my devilish stunts, but I didn't care. All I saw was myself and the excitement of trying new things and wanted her to be a part of it. I begged and begged and eventually lured her up on a tall rooftop one day and convinced her to jump off it onto a branch of a nearby tree. I dared her to do it. I showed her by example and executed the task perfectly. After all, I had lots of experience jumping and playing and challenging myself."

"Did she do it?"

"Yes. But she didn't make it to the tree. She was inexperienced, not so agile, and fell, breaking three of her legs."

The butterfly's eyes lit up with tears.

"And it was all my fault. I knew better."

"Oh, I'm so sorry. Is she okay now?"

"Yes, fortunately. She healed, accepted my apologies, but I never forgave myself for hurting someone I truly loved for my own selfish reasons. I didn't have her back and I caused her great pain. I was broken, destroyed and simply didn't want to live anymore. So I ran away, feeling my children would be better off without me. Feeling the whole world would be better off."

"You did?"

Wow. Jenna could sure relate to that feeling, for she felt the very same.

"Yes. But the king found me, gathered my children together, and led me here so I could heal. In time, I did. I then felt called to spend my life helping others by first taking care of myself and my children. But it took a long time to learn to forgive my daredevil ways and how they had hurt me and others. Eventually I discovered peace and the ability to live in the moment, in faith, not letting my past and future overcome me."

Jenna sat and just stared, taking it all in.

Sometimes when fears and chores and responsibilities wore you down, you forget others have problems too. She was touched that this gentle soul had fought her way back to life after a tragedy and was able to guide others to do the same. She sure hoped she was one of them. She certainly needed lots of direction.

"Thank you for sharing," whispered Jenna. She leaned over to hug the queen. Not so easy when dealing with wings but somehow she managed to do it.

"I want you to know," said the queen, hugging back. "That even in the midst of great crises, new life can begin. Sometimes these horrid experiences bring us to our knees and spiritual enlightenment can take place. It all takes time and making better choices, minute by minute, and as I mentioned before, practice. Look at the caterpillars who shed their skin five times. They evolve and change constantly and move onto the next stage. As you know, the last and final one is the chrysalis where they emerge as a butterfly with total freedom."

"What do you mean by making choices by the minute?"

"Well, as we grow in practicing real living, at any given moment we can choose to be present or filled with fear or anger. We can choose to heal or spend our time mired in hurt and pain. We can choose to see ourselves as we really are, heal, grow, and be our authentic selves or continue to live stagnant, worn down by anxiety."

"It seems so hard though," said Jenna. "I have to admit I have always read about and wanted to be my authentic self. I hear all the time the push to just be *you*, be *yourself* at all times, live your *best* life. But I'm so busy, I forget to focus on what is important. Oh, I know my husband and kids and family but it all just seems so complex. Driving kids everywhere, making money, jobs, housework, dishes. It never ends."

"What about yourself? Do you consider yourself important?"

Pause. Silence.

"Nope. Never."

The queen smiled. "I admire your honesty."

"Well, I'm trying. I do know you are supposed to take care of yourself. I also know that in the Bible when Jesus was asked what the greatest commandment is, He said *to love God and that the second greatest was to love your neighbor as yourself.* I get the trying to take care of others, but really who has time to take care of one's self? I completely ignore myself most of the time."

Once again, surprisingly even shockingly, God appeared in her thoughts.

Imagine remembering lessons from her religion class so long ago.

Guess the mind stores facts and lets them flow when we need them and somehow she felt more spiritual these days. Probably she was remembering Bible passages, due to the intense depth of her self-searching and wanting to live life differently.

Maybe, just maybe, the Bible really did get it right.

If followed, life could be lived in harmony. Maybe?

"I understand ignoring oneself," said the queen. "But as you grow, you simply make time. And you will find that everything else will fall into place. It simply is true. The more you love yourself, the more you have to give to others. You are no longer looking at them through troubled eyes and hearts but clearly focused and seeing truth."

"So easy to say." Jenna sighed. "So hard to understand and harder still to do."

"Yes, it is. That's why it needs to be more than just words and wishful thinking. You really need to live it."

"You're absolutely right. I promise I'll keep trying."

"Only if you choose this way of life, for it has to be your decision. Everyone has their own journey and each path is different, unique only to you. You have to follow yours."

"Thank you. And I do choose this. I crave a sense of stillness as opposed to unnecessary busyness, and you have definitely given me a lot to think about."

"And now I believe Kirby and Shelly need your help back in the kitchen. It's almost time for lunch.

"Thank you." She felt the warm wings around her again as the queen hugged her, then flew away.

Jenna scooted off to the kitchen.

"Hello there," said Kirby. "I heard you had an important job."

"Yes, sure did."

"You should feel honored. The queen only allows special people to help with the chrysalises."

"Yeah, but I messed up. I fell asleep."

"Oh, that's okay." He smiled. "The king and queen watch the room through TV monitors. Nothing bad would ever happen."

Butterflies have TV monitors? Surely he was joking.

"I'm not kidding," he said, laughing at her expression of surprise.

Well. Guess if caterpillars and butterflies could talk, who's to say they couldn't have TV monitors? Wow, this dream was exciting and unbelievably innovative, too. Who knew she had it in her?

"So now come along, Shelly needs help in the dining room."

They hurried over and once again she ate with the caterpillars. This time she observed that a few shed before dinner and a few after. But what she was really interested in was the fact they looked so happy after completing this process. Maybe she should view life like the caterpillar. Shedding her past, as well as any future worries and fears. And maybe, just maybe she would smile like them. With contentment.

Did she miss home?

Yes.

Should she go home?

Yes.

But not quite yet.

She needed to learn more.

She was thirsty to learn more.

They all still had something she wanted.

Seven

"Pay attention, Jenna. Look around you. Breathe in and out. See the light streaming through the tiny openings. Notice how pretty and soothing it is. Feel the floor under your feet. Breathe in and out. Hear your footsteps. Note that your shoulders hurt a bit this morning. Watch those caterpillars bringing leaves to the kitchen. Observe their serene faces. Breathe in and out."

"Are you talking to yourself, Miss Jenna?" asked an obviously concerned Kirby, joining her as she walked down the hall. "Is something wrong?"

"Pardon? Oh, was I talking out loud?" Jenna could feel her face turn red. She hadn't even realized she was doing this and also didn't know Kirby was nearby. Yikes. So much for being alert and aware.

"Um, yes."

"Oh."

He looked puzzled.

"Well, so now you know my secret," said Jenna. "I have a hard time focusing on the present and it amazes me how I can walk around noticing nothing except inner thoughts filled with anxiety. So I talk to myself, usually not out loud though, and point out stuff around me.

Somehow this helps keep me focused and hopefully eventually it will become second nature."

"Oh. Sounds like a great idea."

Jenna laughed. "Not sure if it really is but it seems to work for me. I tend to get so wrapped up in my past and my future and let fear, uncertainty and regrets flood me. So much so, I pay no attention at all to the moment I'm in. I simply let it pass me by."

"Then by all means, go for it. Do whatever it takes."

"Do you find it hard living in the present?"

"Of course. Everyone does, Miss Jenna. It takes lots of practice and meeting each challenge head on. But it's the best way to live ever. To be clear-headed, free and at peace rocks. And if I can do it, so can you."

"You really think so?"

He grinned, tipping his hat. "I know so."

She curtsied back, loving the grand gesture with the hat, loving their special moments of fun and silliness.

"Well, thank you, kind sir. Thanks for your vote of confidence. I appreciate it."

"Always. Are you off to the chrysalis room?"

"Of course."

"Great to see you so devoted."

"I love it."

"Good. Nice to find a passion. Well, I'll see you later."

Kirby turned off at the kitchen while Jenna continued to the special room. She walked in and looked around. It felt different somehow.

Oh, my goodness.

Did something move?

In one of the sacs?

She bopped her head back and forth, searching each one in anticipation. No more movement. Maybe it had just been her imagination.

She settled back in her chair.

Jenna spent most of her days watching them.

Every morning after breakfast she raced to this room, longing and hoping to see a butterfly emerge. In fact, she couldn't wait to get there, not wanting to miss anything, sometimes even taking breakfast to go. That was, until Kirby caught her sneaking off one day.

"No way," he had said, shaking his head. "Being part of a community is very important. I thought your absences were part of the queen's plan but found out it was just your own idea. You need to dine with us. It's part of our life here of support for one another."

He was right. Lost in her own world she was isolating herself. Just like she did in her own family, immersing herself on her cell phone right at the dinner table, ignoring her children, not to mention her husband. But she so loved this room.

It had become her happy spot, her safe place, a quiet, soothing, healing space just to be. Never again did she fall asleep on duty for she had come to treasure these special moments. If this was what meditation was all about, she should have started the practice years ago. Her mind was beginning to quiet. She was less frantic and panicky. Her thoughts weren't twisting and turning all over the pace and her fears and anxiety were dwindling away. Slowly but surely. She was listening more to her heart and she was seeing the world as it was, not the way she wanted it to be or tried to make it be.

She had even begun to pray, which absolutely stunned her for she hadn't done that in years and years.

She was actually kind of liking it. She was trusting again, growing in faith and peace.

The chrysalis room was also the perfect place to develop badly needed observational tools, for these chrysalises depended on her. She had to be alert to keep them safe.

Wait a second.

Did something move again?

Inside one of the chrysalises?

It was just a flicker but enough to get her excited again, for she was sure this time it was reality, not her imagination.

She stood and moved closer, keeping her eyes glued to the precious sac.

Yes. Movement. For sure. It was finally going to happen. She backed up saying quietly, so as not to disturb the goings on, "King, queen. A chrysalis is hatching. I believe a butterfly is trying to get free."

She knew they were listening and watching the monitors and felt she needed them there in case she messed up. She was so nervous she was calling in reinforcements, no longer ashamed to ask for help when needed. It was a lesson she had to learn, for in her previous world she often tried to do everything herself and look where that got her. Nowhere.

Besides, this was her first. Her first time seeing a butterfly emerge. Goosebumps rose on her arms. She was so excited.

The king and queen flew in almost immediately. Guess when you can fly, you can get there mighty fast.

They radiated an aura of serenity and stability as they quickly went over and inspected the chrysalis. Feeling caught up in their capable hands, Jenna relaxed. Well, they didn't have hands, so she couldn't really use that adage. Caught up in their antennae maybe? Yeah, that would work.

"Good eyes." The queen smiled. "I think you are right. It's time."

"Yayyyy," whispered Jenna, thrilled beyond her wildest belief. "It's going to be soon, right?"

The king took a long look as well.

"Yes. Definitely."

The queen smiled. "Be prepared to witness a miracle."

Jenna moved a ladder closer and climbed up to get the best possible look.

She watched intently, wanting to treasure each second.

Suddenly, the chrysalis started to shake.

She leaned forward to watch the butterfly wiggle around. Then slowly, carefully, bit by bit, it began to break through its enclosure. She held her breath as she witnessed it emerge—the big long antennae, head, legs, body—and she released her breath in a gush of joy as the wings popped out, free and intact.

Breathtaking, with no problems whatsoever.

Alleluia.

But she was so glad the king and queen were there, just in case.

Now, was it a boy or a girl butterfly?

She had learned that the male had two black oval markings on its hind wing. The female didn't.

She scanned the wings. It was a girl, who held onto the remnants of her chrysalis, as if savoring the moment. Jenna admired how her wings glistened like shiny diamonds. Their wetness added a glowing ethereal effect that almost took her breath away again.

"Oh, wow. This is beautiful," she whispered. "You're right. It's a miracle of heavenly proportions."

Everything about this process was truly magnificent.

She could feel her eyes grow wider and she was sure they were glowing as well as she recalled the first time she had held Ellie, then Jason. That feeling was very similar. After all she'd been monitoring and anticipating the butterfly's safe arrival for what seemed like ages. Another birth in her life.

The king and queen smiled, seemingly delighted at her joy.

"Yes, it truly is one of nature's wonders," said the queen.

"When will she start flying?"

"It takes a bit of time," said the king. "She needs to pump oxygen throughout her body and dry her wings. She needs to be ready. Butterflies don't rush the process and eventually know when to take on the ultimate challenge of flying."

Needed to be ready.

Didn't we all.

She envied the beautiful creature, wishing she could do the same in her own life, as once again it hit her how often she rushed things, tried to make life happen, pushed too hard when she probably should have waited for the right moment to make a move. She was also always trying to fix things, make sure everyone was doing okay, all the while worrying and flooding herself with fears. She had messed up her life. One thing was for sure...she wasn't good at making things better at all and that was probably why her children were messed up as well. Or at least her son. She really did need to heal and sort out all the crazy stuff going on inside herself that made her like this. Only then would she be any good to others.

Was this even attainable? It was a question that shot out over and over.

She glanced at the queen's peaceful face. She really hoped so.

Once again, she gave thanks for the experience of being in this beautiful community. Dream or not, it was just what she needed. Too bad Milkweed Manor wasn't a school that everyone had to visit and stay a while to learn the real truth about how to live. She just hoped she graduated one day, and rejoined her family.

Please, God, please let this happen.

Once again, she was praying. Odd, but still happening, and a welcomed experience in her life. Who would have ever figured that?

Jenna continued to watch, anticipating the moment the butterfly would take its first flight.

Silence. Quiet. Solitude.

Little by little, Jenna could tell the butterfly was growing stronger.

She was also fascinated at how the king and queen presided over their charges. Jenna noticed their eyes never left the new hatchling until suddenly...ever so gently, the butterfly tried out its wings, slowly flapping them, until finally pushing away and confidently flying up into the air and out through the hole.

She was gone. In a moment.

Jenna climbed down the ladder, instantly feeling empty.

She turned to stare at the king and queen, tears dripping down her face.

"You are sad, Jenna. But please believe this is truly a glorious moment," said the queen. "The caterpillar has achieved its final transformation and is beginning a new freer life, better than he or she could ever imagine."

"Yes," said the king. "It is a time of soaring into the heavens. Living life in all one's glory."

Soaring into the heavens, thought Jenna. Living life in magnificent glory. How beautifully said.

She locked eyes with the queen.

"Will I soar into the heavens one day?"

"Yes, dear. One day you too may soar. Humans do it a bit differently though, but the end result is the same."

"Yeah. Guess we can't spin a chrysalis." Jenna grinned.

"Not like us but just as good."

"How?"

"One day you will know."

"So you're not sad when each butterfly flies away? I'm already dreading the day my children leave home. I guess it doesn't look like it since I don't want to go back home, but I really am."

"It is pure joy," said the king. "To raise our charges to evolve and awaken to all life is, makes everything worthwhile. Our job is not to hold them back, but to send them forward."

"Yes, I agree with the king," said the queen. "Like parents, we do not own them but are just their caretakers for a while. When I see them fly away, I am truly happy, knowing I did what I was meant to do in terms of raising them, and they have successfully moved on, taking with them all the wisdom they hopefully learned from us."

Silence.

Jenna took in all they were saying.

After a few moments, the queen said, "How are you doing lately?"

"I'm okay."

And she really was, at least for right now, still touched by this beautiful experience and understanding its significance.

"You mentioned your children. How are you feeling about them?" asked the queen.

"Well, I miss Ellie and Jason lots. More and more each day. But I'm learning so much here. So many things that are helping me and hopefully will help them one day."

"Glad to hear that."

"I just worry that I am overstaying my welcome. May I continue to stay longer or do you want me to leave?"

"Yes, of course, you may stay," said the king. "You are welcomed here for as long as you feel the need. You've also been a big help to us."

"Thank you." Jenna basked in the praise.

"We just want what's best for you, little one," said the queen. "And we are always here for you."

With that, she and the king flew away.

Jenna still giggled when they occasionally called her little one. She knew it was just a sign of their affection…after all she was small compared to them, but considering she was definitely in the overweight classification based on her height and poundage, being called little was not usual in the least.

On the other hand, she kind of liked it.

Usually she referred to herself as hideously obese and had been teased numerous times over the years, just based on how she looked. She'd been called a blimp, a whale, and probably every horrid fat name around. She hated how she looked, obviously so did bullies, but could never seem to stop overeating.

Until now.

Yes, she had a secret.

One she was excited about.

She was losing weight.

Surprisingly, after years and years of dieting and gaining and dieting and gaining and starving herself and later pigging out, she found herself losing. Without even trying. It was pretty confusing but pretty wonderful all at the same time. Here she was not even thinking of calories or cutting down or how many carbs she'd ingested and if she'd eaten enough protein.

So just why were the pounds sliding off?

She sat back down to reflect.

Hmmmmm…

Guess feeling calmer ended the wildly emotional stress eating, but it was more than that.

It had to be love. As the queen said, love was the basis of everything good.

A growing, albeit slowly, love of self.

Jenna found she was actually starting to care for herself in a new world where no one was critical, not even herself. Or at least she was learning not to. Losing some weight seemed to also be a by-product of living here, where no one ever made fun of anyone else or called out hurtful names based on someone's physical appearance.

The caterpillars and the king and queen were consistently positive and upbeat, and it was unbelievably refreshing. She was learning to like herself all over again, to not beat herself up all the time, or disapprove so much that it sent her right to the fridge to shove cake down her throat to stuff her feelings away. Of course, there no fridges here or cake, but she did have a stash of chocolate and cookies that she rarely touched. She no longer wanted to hurt herself with all the empty eating she used to do when she was not hungry in the least. She was tired of that Ferris wheel of going round and round, eating too much, feeling sick, having horrible indigestion and doing it all over again. And hating herself for that endless, tedious way of living.

Plus, she was no longer playing games with her health. Oh, the games dieters play. She knew them all. Her head spun remembering all the times she'd break her diet, eat enough to feed a small country, always promising that tomorrow she'd begin again. Or the days she'd use extreme self-control to stay away from fattening foods until one day she gave in and couldn't stop chowing down on sugar. And then there were all the hiding places she had for her continual mound of endless snacks. An old hat box for example, stuffed in the corner of her closet, held a storefront of chocolate.

Now, she felt healthy for a change.

There are no limits here, the queen had said. She was right. She was no longer putting off living her life until she was thin, not even thinking about it as a matter of fact, not even longing that it would make a difference and almost unknowingly, pounds were slipping off. Guess she was now more focused on the journey, not the end result.

Just out of curiosity, Jenna wondered if anyone else had noticed. Probably not. Her clothes were baggy to begin with and covered her loosening waist band, but guess it really didn't matter because *she* knew and that was all that mattered.

Another thing to remember—the fact that she couldn't control what other people thought, only herself.

So much wisdom to garner.

Another benefit of being at Milkweed Manor.

For the first time she realized that just maybe, peace seemed attainable.

And real love.

Beginning with herself.

She hoped it continued.

Because it sure felt good.

Eight

Jenna couldn't wait to tell Kirby her good news.

Relieved of her duties by another caterpillar, she hurried to the kitchen looking for her buddy. If she'd had wings, she would have flown. She couldn't contain her excitement.

"Guess what?" she said, running over to him.

"Well, your eyes are glittering and you're smiling, so it must be good news. Um, I give up. What?"

"I finally saw a butterfly emerge."

"You did?"

"Yes. It was truly glorious. One of the best things I've ever seen. Ever."

"Sure is."

Jenna couldn't help herself.

Suffused with joy, she started doing a little victory dance, waving her arms and moving her feet to the beat of her heart.

To her thrill, Kirby joined in.

They made quite the odd dance partners. A tiny human and a large caterpillar bopping a silly jig.

It was just about perfect.

"Still can't believe I witnessed a complete metamorphosis," said Jenna coming to a stop, panting, but still giggling away. "And I hope I see more of this."

"I'm sure you will. And maybe we can even perfect our little happy dance along the way." He laughed.

"Yeah, that was fun. Didn't know you had those moves in you."

"I love to dance but hey, I was looking for you, too. Wanna go for another ride or are you too tired?"

"Tired? Are you kidding? I'd love to. I have a ton of energy to burn. A ride is just what I need."

This time she was prepared for the trek down the milkweed stem and Kirby's stop at the bottom.

She looked up.

"Hey, the little caterpillar is out of its shell and eating it."

"Sure is. Another new one added to our community. Soon it will join us in the dining room, craving milkweed leaves."

"Wonderful. And one more future butterfly."

"For sure."

As they began their stroll through the grass, Jenna found herself still happy as anything and marveled at the wonders she was seeing first hand. She was one lucky girl, she thought, as she glanced around, completely unprepared by how delightful everything looked. It was if all the plants and flowers, including the grass, were bright and glowing, paying homage to a special day. A day a new butterfly found its freedom.

At the same time, she was puzzled.

"Have things changed?" she asked.

"Ah, no. What makes you think it has?"

"Well, everything looks brighter, more colorful, stunningly beautiful. Just look at those tulips. Their reds and oranges are so vibrant, it's almost blinding."

Kirby laughed. "It's not your surroundings that have changed."

"What do you mean?"

"Well, you've changed. You are noticing things, seeing them in a different light. When your life becomes more peaceful and you begin to live in the present, you see clearly without all your worries and fears clouding your eyes. You're looking through a clear lens now, not misty, gloomy ones."

"Really?"

"Really."

Jenna gazed around, taking stock of how she felt, and discovered she was definitely feeling calmer for even longer stretches these days. Used to be she'd feel it for a few minutes here and there; now it was lasting.

"Oh my goodness. I think you're right."

Her eyes opened wider as she feasted on anything and everything. Without allowing terror to conquer her, marring her vision, she was way more alert, just like Kirby said.

It truly was amazing.

Another miracle.

When was the last time she had even noticed a flower and been stunned by its vibrancy? Or the shimmering color of the sky and grass? Ages, that was for sure. Definitely not since a kid, when she was fascinated with dandelions and would lay in the grass for hours on warm summer days, smelling them, touching them.

"Oops, would you mind getting down for a minute?" asked Kirby urgently, coming to a dramatic stop.

"What? Oh, okay." Jenna pulled herself out of her haze of joy and hopped down.

What was Kirby doing?

He moved a few feet away, tugged, pulled, wiggled and suddenly his skin seemed to just fall right off him.

"Why, you're shedding." She moved closer, intrigued.

He grinned. "Sure am."

"Does it hurt?"

"Nope, not at all."

She watched until it was over and the spark of enjoyment in Kirby's eyes touched her heart.

"So it feels good?" she asked.

"Incredible. It's a visible sign of growth and shows that I have reached a new level. I'm thrilled. But don't mind me. I need to eat it now. Don't forget, it's part of the process of how we do this."

"Sure, I remember. Go ahead."

She continued to watch, fascinated. Her friend Kirby had moved into a newer level in his life and, lucky girl, she got to observe the transformation. It was truly an honor.

"Finished," he shouted with glee. "So let's get going. Hop back on and we'll continue."

She did, thinking, *would she ever shed?*

Could she?

Well maybe not like he did, she would never be shedding her real skin, unless you counted the pounds she had dropped, but figuratively?

Had she really changed?

Could she?

She sure hoped so. She was loving the fact she could see more clearly and was even losing some weight. Maybe when she cracked the mystery of Milkweed Manor, she might make more progress and become even healthier. She sure hoped so. It was worth the stay if enlightenment was the end result.

She prayed it was.

They quickly traveled through the rest of the bright green grass, up the tree and over to the deck.

"Back to my house again?"

"Yes, this is my daily route. I even keep an eye on your family."

"Thank you."

She'd been so excited; she'd forgotten to ask where they were going. Not sure she would have come, knowing their destination. On the other hand, it might be good to see her son again. Maybe he'd look great and be the sunny, happy boy she always thought he was. Maybe the last time was just a fluke, an awful product of her imagination.

Still, guilt surged through her.

Imagine a caterpillar watching out for her family and not herself? Now how bizarre was that?

"You'd let me know if something bad happened, right?" she asked.

"Sure would. And besides, we needed to come back here; you're getting low on peanut butter."

"Oh, okay."

Amazing how he continually looked out for her, for she hadn't noticed her wares were decreasing to the point they needed a refill. Probably because she wasn't as obsessed with food like before. Hopefully, that was the truth, but she couldn't help being afraid as they drew nearer.

"Um, I'm not going to have another revelation moment, am I?" she asked. "Like the last time?"

"Not that I know of," said Kirby. "I just do what I need to do and gathering more food for you is my goal right now."

Jenna heaved in a huge intake of breath and let it out.

Here goes, she thought, as they sneaked in the side door. Guess it wasn't really sneaking since Jenna was part owner.

She looked around, stopped in her tracks, as her heart sped up.

Her children were in the kitchen.

To be honest, she was really hoping to not run into any family members but no such luck. Jason was doing his homework again at the table and Ellie was grabbing something out of the fridge. Jenna was still amazed that Jason worked there. He literally must flee to his room when she arrived home. Sigh. Probably to avoid her. But really? Could she blame him?

She noted his too long hair again, too small clothes and how worried he looked. Yep, he really was this dishevelled and stressed, it was not her imagination. Nothing had changed since the last time she saw him. Once again she struggled to acknowledge the fact she had missed all of this.

She next turned her attention to her daughter, Ellie, almost afraid of what she'd see.

Wow.

She was right to be fearful.

What had happened to her?

She was pale, her hair stringy and unkempt, tied back in a loose ponytail, strands escaping the scrunchie.

Was she always like this and once again, Jenna hadn't noticed?

Bet she was. This couldn't have happened overnight.

What kind of mother never really saw her own kids for who they were?

This question circled her mind again, speeding up like a merry-go-round whirling, twirling around and around.

The realization that she was the worst mother ever sliced through her again.

"Don't worry. We'll sneak by them," said Kirby.

"Thanks."

Guess he sensed her tense up. Once again, she really admired how it seemed as if everyone at Milkweed Manor was sensitive to everyone else's moods and well-being. It was truly amazing and she continually wished this gift would rub off on her. In time, maybe it would. Hoped so.

Kirby hurried her to the other side of the kitchen and up on the counter, where he encouraged her to grab some more bread along with the peanut butter. Her children didn't notice. But then again, Jenna had never seen Kirby there and apparently he was there all the time.

She stopped in her tracks when her children started talking.

Should she listen?

Yes.

She might find out something she needed to know and besides she was curious about what they were saying. Sure it was eavesdropping but Scrooge seemed to learn from his excursions. Since this was the second time something similar had happened to her, she figured she had borrowed these dream scenarios from the movie she'd probably seen at least twenty times; it being one of Scott's favorites. Watching from afar. Not a bad way to sort her life out and learn from her errors. Scrooge sure figured it out. So could she. Maybe?

Her children's conversation sounded just like chitchat at first, about sports and school, until all of a sudden Jason raised his voice.

"You have to tell Mom."

Wait. Was Jason yelling? At his sister? Usually they got along well. Or at least she'd thought so.

"No. And don't you tell her either," screamed Ellie.

Jenna, who was hiding behind the toaster again, leaned out to watch. She was surprised her daughter yelled back. She'd rarely even heard her raise her voice either, especially to her brother. As far as she knew, this was odd behavior between the both of them.

"Well, tell Dad then," said Jason.

"No."

Tell us what?

"You don't get it, they'll notice soon enough."

Notice what?

"No, they won't." Ellie shut the fridge door. "They're too busy to see anything but their cell phones."

Ouch, that hurt. A lot. Especially since it appeared to be true.

"But you're getting too skinny."

What?

Losing weight? Her daughter was losing weight?

Once again, Jenna had never even noticed.

Ellie had always been a bit chubby and come to think of it, wore her school uniform, plaid kilt and white blouse, baggy and loose. She completed the ensemble with a long black sweater that flowed over everything, but she had always seemed fine to Jenna.

Guilt hit hard. Again.

Was Ellie hiding a serious problem?

She also faced the fact that it was her fault about any weight gains. Since she went back to work, most of their meals were take-out or hastily slopped together with no regard to good nutrition or being healthy. She'd gained weight herself eating lousy full fat, high salt concoctions. It wasn't just stress eating. It was what she put in her mouth at family meals, as well, simply not caring.

But what about good nutrition for her family?

Once again, she had failed them.

Staring at her daughter, she scanned her head to toe, checking her out. She squinted, trying to imagine her body under the loose clothing.

Yes, she really did look thinner.

Not in a good, healthy way, either.

Jenna had already noticed her daughter's auburn hair looked drab and lackluster, but now she got a good look at her face. It was whiter by the minute, her freckles stood out shockingly and her eyes appeared huge in her leaner face. Wrinkles had even surfaced on her cheeks. Was she on some kind of diet? Did she feel pressure to be thin? Odd. Because she sure seemed to eat, at least at supper time.

Was she sick?

Was that why Jason looked worried?

"No, they won't notice," shouted Ellie. "I'm careful and no way am I too skinny."

Careful? About what?

"You are too skinny and you're not as careful as you think. I heard you puking in the bathroom last night and I Googled your symptoms. You're bulimic, aren't you?"

Bulimic? Her daughter was bulimic?

"I am not."

"Yes, you are. You eat normally in front of us, then get sick. And you wear baggy clothes to hide your body. That's why no one notices. I wouldn't either except the bathroom is next to my room and I hear you, even though you try to cover it up with music. Don't lie to me. I'm on your side. I just don't want you to get really sick. Mom and Dad are always busy." His voice quavered with emotion. "You're all I have."

Jenna grimaced. His words were a knife to the heart but ones she deserved. He was right. His parents *were* always busy. That was probably why her children seemed to get along so well. They stuck together.

Sadness hit her hard as she watched her daughter sit down, head in hands, looking the picture of sadness.

Silence, stillness then... "Yeah, you're right. Please don't tell."

Oh, no. It was true? Her daughter was bulimic? And she even admitted it?

Jenna doubled over in pain.

How was it that Ellie was in huge trouble also and once again it had slipped on by her?

She wasn't surprised her daughter told her brother the truth for they had always been close. But how shocking that her son noticed the problem and she hadn't.

Shhhhh.... Calm your mind. Your son is speaking again.

"I won't say anything, because *you* are. I'll give you one week to tell Mom or Dad."

"No way, they will freak out." Ellie was staring at her brother, her face a picture of fear.

"Too bad. You have to do this. You need help."

Her daughter hung her head. Seconds ticked by.

"Well, okay," she finally said, raising her head. "You leave me no choice. Maybe Dad, though. Mom's too busy. Too stressed."

Oh, no. There was that stressed and too busy comment again. Seemed like it was all they noticed about her and unfortunately they were absolutely right. Her kids were experiencing huge problems and she had been blissfully unaware, completely wrapped up in her own issues, pretending she was following her dreams and giving them a good example of how to do so. Instead, she was showing them how to walk through life ignoring others and worrying all the time about yourself. Not only had she gotten off track, she'd forged a new trail of neglect and all she had revealed to them was how to disregard their needs and the needs of others. Some mother she was. Once again, the worst, ever.

"Well, I have to go," said Jason, rolling his eyes. "Basketball practice."

"I'll make you a deal," said Ellie. "I'll come clean about my eating problem if you'll tell Mom and Dad how much you hate basketball."

He looked horrified, shook his head as if to protest, seemed like he was thinking about it, then quickly said, "Okay, it's a deal. Anything to help you."

"Pinky swear?" Ellie held out her baby finger.

"Pinky swear." Jason clasped her finger with his and they made a pact, the same way they'd been doing since they were toddlers.

He picked up his books, left, and a few minutes later so did his sister, sucking back water from the bottle she'd taken out of the fridge.

"Are you okay for now?" asked Kirby.

"Yes," said Ellie.

Bulimic?

Jenna still couldn't get over it.

Was her daughter going to die?

She had to get out of there.

No, she should stay.

Her children needed her.

But she was still completely overwhelmed by all she had missed in their lives.

An eating disorder?

That could be deadly?

Was it real? Or part of the nightmare imaginary aspect of this crazy dream she was lodged in?

Panic struck. She started to shake.

She was sure it was all real and yes, she had to go.

She was a coward.

She needed to get out of there fast.

To absorb what she had heard.

To face the fact anew about how little she really knew about her children. Not to mention that once again all she could think about was that they were better off without her. She was one lousy guide in their lives. Basically, showing them nothing positive about how to communicate and cope with life.

She swung right back into a state of depression. All the gains she had been making flew out the window.

Depression, her old friend, descended upon her like it never left.

She wondered how long she had been so sad.

It certainly seemed a state she was way too familiar with, making it easy to slip back into.

Maybe she had felt this way her whole life.

"I want to go," she said firmly. The noise in her head was loud, unbearably loud. She had to get away. Now.

"You're sure?" asked Kirby, concern reflected in his eyes.

"Yes. My children certainly don't need me."

"I think you're wrong."

"No. I know I'm right. Let's go."

"Well, okay. If that's what you want."

"It is."

She jumped on his back and held on tight as he took off, tears rolling down her cheeks.

"Do you want to talk about it?" Kirby asked after a few minutes.

"No, thanks."

"Well, I'm always here if you need me."

"Yeah, thanks. I know this and I appreciate it."

Sometimes you just needed to be with a friend. Not necessarily to talk but just for comfort. Kirby was very soothing to Jenna. His presence was familiar and calm and reassuring. But once again, she couldn't find the words to tell him all that was bothering her.

It sure looked like she was never going back to her real home.

She had failed.

Big time.

Her family simply didn't need her self-centered brand of love.

Once again she concluded, they'd be better off without her.

And she was never going to get over it.

Nine

Jenna eased out of sleep and slowly opened her eyes.

Something was different.

She touched her face.

Get out.

She was smiling?

Yep, her lips were curving upward.

For the first time in absolute ages she had greeted the morning with a grin. She couldn't even remember when the last time was. Years ago probably.

What was making her so happy?

Why, she even felt somewhat peaceful.

"Excuse me, Jenna. Are you awake?"

She sat up. It was the queen's voice.

"May I come in?"

"Oh sure."

Jenna jumped out of bed just as the queen floated into the room. She was shimmering with light and her eyes were glowing more than ever. Jenna looked around the room. As a matter of fact, the whole room was bright, bathed in golds and reds, as if on fire. Of course, there were no flames, everything was just gleaming.

What was going on?

"Why is it so bright in here?" she asked, confused.

"It's not." The queen smiled. "At least no more than usual. But you look radiant and it tells me that you are seeing the world differently now. It happens. You view it as much brighter than the dark space it once appeared to you."

Her words were very similar to what Kirby had said yesterday on the way to her house.

Wait a second.

"I look radiant?"

"Yes."

"Really? Well, I think *you* are glowing."

She smiled. "Only in your eyes."

"So, it really is because I see the world differently now?"

"Yes, definitely."

"Well, I sure feel good. Really good. I even woke up with a smile."

Her daughter Ellie's face suddenly marched across her mind. It was like a painful, totally unexpected slap across the cheek, and it brought her to her knees.

Oh, no.

It was all coming back to her.

How had she forgotten?

"Are you all right?" asked the queen. "Your face has suddenly gone white."

"No, I'm not. I just remembered something. And there is absolutely no reason I should be smiling," she said, an old familiar haunting sadness taking up residence again.

The queen looked concerned as Jenna watched her flutter closer.

"The real reason I came to see you," she said, "is because Kirby said you had a rough day yesterday. And here I find you looking the best ever. Or at least, you were."

Confusion swirled around Jenna.

"Yeah, well, it sure seems kind of crazy to have been so happy a minute ago. Kirby was right. Yesterday was horrible. The worst yet."

She closed her eyes.

The image of her daughter looking sickly, as well as Jason looking unkempt, burned through her brain.

Shaking her head, she started to tremble.

A good part of her confusion was the fact she still felt so muddled, not knowing if what she saw was real or just manifested in her dream world.

Nevertheless, remembering what she saw tormented her.

Jenna was thankful that the queen stayed quiet, once again giving her time to find her words because yes, she really did want to talk to this beautiful butterfly about what she was going through. She stood up. She needed help.

"I'm a lousy mother, Queen, there is no way around it. I never noticed that my daughter has an eating disorder and once again I ran away, not wanting to deal with it. I felt overwhelmed, scared and full of fear, obviously thinking more of my own pain than my daughter's. I'm disgusted with my selfish, selfish self."

"I'm sorry to hear about your daughter and how upset you are."

"But...you know, it's strange. I was really a mess last night and for hours I felt lost, devastated, empty, depressed." Immersed in her yesterday, Jenna spoke slowly, thinking out loud, struggling to put the pieces together. One minute she was upset, the next happy, the next sad and so on. It was crazy. "I considered running. Going far, far away and never coming back, believing my whole family is better off without me. That I had ruined them." A tear floated down her cheek. "But..." She raised her eyes to stare at the queen, acknowledging to herself that she was in shock. "Then something amazing happened."

"Oh? What?"

"Well, in the midst of feeling guilty and upset with myself, hating who I am, and my heart breaking over how troubled my children are, I also realized that I had lost all the serenity I had gained, as well as all the lessons I was learning here. So after crying my heart out for what seemed like ages, I started to pray."

Silence.

Jenna continued to lock eyes with the queen, basking in her compassion.

"So get that. Amazing. Me? Praying? I still can't get over the fact I have been doing this, bit by bit, since arriving here. Still not as much as I should be doing, though. Frankly I feel guilty asking God to help me. After all, I had walked away from my children who needed love and care. I don't deserve any heavenly help at all."

"This is when you need it the most," said the queen, softly, gently. "And God will always be there for you."

"Yeah, I see that now. And I also remembered your words. You said the first thing to do is to step back and acknowledge and accept how I feel. So I managed to calm myself down enough to try this, as if I were just observing myself from a distance, and admitted what I witnessed and how I felt. I faced my own truths and to be honest, it was hard to do. Still is. They are not pretty. But the important thing is that I allowed myself to feel what I was feeling without trying to overeat or ignore my thoughts or lock them away or rationalize myself out of them. I also tried to keep my mind from twirling with all sorts of ideas and possible solutions. Surprisingly, I felt a tiny seedling of love emerge, so I then prayed for healing and cried myself to sleep. And then, hey, I woke up smiling. Go figure."

"Looks like you experienced some healing."

"Really? Do you think that's what's going on? And why I feel sort of okay? Even in the midst of chaos and sadness?"

"What do you think?"

"Well, I tried hard not to overreact, as well as not fall into old traps of immersing myself in fear and endless scenarios where I beat myself up and hurt myself even more. I tried to love myself in the midst of great pain. But it was difficult facing how blind I've been to everyone in my family. That I was surrounded by children who are suffering and I never noticed or acknowledged them. I ignored my own pain, too."

Her tears poured out again.

When she was all cried out, the queen said, "Loving yourself, even in the midst of great torment and pain is definitely key. You were wise to try to do this."

"Me? Wise? I doubt it but you know, I do feel lighter somehow and now I seem to see the world so much brighter, clearer. Like I've lost a huge, heavy weight off my shoulders. It truly is as if, even in the midst of a difficult time, a crisis, a horrid situation, I still feel all right, grounded, together, able to cope and wanting to accept myself but also grow and change. Or at least allow the real me to come out."

A thought flew through her.

"Hey, it's almost like I shed a layer of skin like Kirby did yesterday."

The butterfly smiled. "I think you're getting it."

"Getting what?" she asked.

"You'll see."

"Do you think the better I feel about myself, the more I forgive myself and learn from the ways I sabotage myself and really don't like myself, the more I will be able to help my daughter when I feel ready? In short, the more I love myself, the more I can really love her? And help her?"

"Yes, I do. She will learn by your caring example."

"But when will I know it's time to go home? If ever. My mind still says go. My heart says no."

"You will know."

"Yeah. So you keep telling me." Jenna grinned. "Will you kick me out when you feel I should leave?"

The queen smiled. "No, Jenna. It will be your decision. There will be no kicking out."

With that, she floated away.

Jenna understood.

No one could really tell her when she was healed or when to leave.

One day she really would know, she at least hoped so.

Meanwhile, she needed to continue to practice what she was learning. Yes, her heart broke when she thought of her children's problems, but she still first needed to figure herself out, to feel at one with herself, before she could help them. She needed to be a butterfly to them, like the queen was to her, and she was far from that at the moment. Surely in time, she could do this by getting rid of her blinders and narrow focus about life. Where once she thought she was actually helping her children, in fact, she was unaware of who they really were, what they were experiencing and what they really needed. She had to fix herself before she could help anyone else. Considering all the pain she had caused them, that was now a given.

And she was determined to do so.

Eager to begin another day of learning, she quickly got ready and hurried to the kitchen to find Kirby.

"You look fantastic," he said, as Jenna entered the room.

"I feel it too. I think I really am changing and for the better."

"I think you are too. But I sure was worried about you yesterday."

"Yeah, I was too. Seeing my daughter and what she's going through, made me feel I had lost all the progress I'd made here. I slipped back into a dark hole but managed to climb out of it again. And I want to thank you for being such a good friend by just being there for me. It was exactly what I needed."

She reached out to give him a hug.

"I think I really am continually seeing things clearer now," she added. "My mind isn't churning around with crazy thoughts anymore or at least I'm able to stop them. I'm not trying to mend things all the time and I'm acknowledging how I am feeling instead of running from my problems or eating them by stuffing myself with food. Hey, I've even lost some weight."

"Yes." He grinned, standing back, watching her. "I noticed."

"You have?"

"Of course. Everyone here has."

"And you never said anything?"

"Yes, I did. I told you that you looked beautiful every time I saw you. I never mentioned your weight because I love you no matter how much you weigh. I accept you and want *you* to feel accepted at every moment of your growth."

"Really? Why thank you."

So Kirby accepted her no matter how much she weighed. She did others, too. So she wondered why she was always so hard on herself, berating herself constantly about how fat she was. Definitely something to change. Another adjustment in her life, for sure.

Loving and accepting herself was still so new to her.

She kept thinking she always had to improve, be thin and almost perfect before she could even make an attempt to respect herself. It was sure a different way of living when you chose to love yourself, flaws and all, instead of beating yourself up. The more she mastered this, the more she could be there for her family. Or at least she hoped so.

Was her family in trouble?

She was still unsure about what was real and what wasn't.

Or was it just her fear surfacing? Trying to rob her of everything? Making her see the world in fuzzy depressing terms? Distracting her from living in peace.

"Only you can figure out your journey with food," said Kirby, jumping into Jenna's thoughts. "Try not to be hassled by other's standards. And always remember that you are beautiful at every stage of your development. Most of all, you don't have to be perfect. No one is."

"I agree in theory, but it's sure hard to accept. I've always had eating issues."

"Looks like you connect stress with overeating."

"I sure do," said Jenna. "I've always lived in anger about my weight, trying diet after diet, starving and binging. But somehow, now I care enough not to hurt myself by stuffing food down my throat. I'm even trying to eat healthier. Living in the present, or trying to, is really changing me."

"It's the best way to live. It has changed all of us here."

"Will it last?"

"With practice, yes. It takes time. A lifetime. We are all so used to living stressed out and filled with worry and fear and anxiety. But eventually we can begin living the way life is meant to be experienced. Perceptive and in the moment only."

"Well, I'm going to keep trying every day. I love the way I feel and the way I am now beginning to view the world so differently."

If only she could help her family. That is, if her family really needed help. Tucked away in the back of her mind, she still hoped it was all just a dream. Because as far as she was concerned, super large caterpillars didn't exist and she really couldn't be living in a Milkweed. Right?

"Well, speaking of changing, I have something I want to talk to you about."

"Okay," said Jenna. "More rides? Please, no more rides for a while." She laughed. "But of course, if you need some company, I'll be there. Anything for you. You're always here for me."

Sure wished she'd said this to her children and husband. Maybe she had, but she really didn't mean it. Often she viewed doing things for them as total pressure and one more chore to get through. And here she was willing to be there for her friend without even having to think about it.

Whew.

This honest self search was shocking. Owning up to her weaknesses was eye-opening and certainly not very flattering.

But definitely necessary.

Kirby smiled. "No, it's not about rides. Please, follow me."

Jenna did, excited, confused, but eager to be there for her buddy.

The way he always was for her.

Ten

Surprisingly, Kirby led her straight to the chrysalis room

"You're staying with me today?" asked Jenna, surprised. Usually his main job was in the kitchen. She'd never even heard him talk about watching butterflies emerge.

"Not exactly. It's just that it's my turn."

"Your turn?"

"Yes."

"For what? I'm here, you don't have to stay."

"Yes, I do. It's my turn to fly."

"What do you mean?"

"Think about it." He grinned.

Jenna did, staring into his expressive eyes, acknowledging that he seemed pretty excited about something.

She got it.

How had she been so slow figuring this out?

"No way. You're becoming a butterfly?"

"Yes."

"But of course. You're a caterpillar. I forgot this would happen to you one day."

Part of her was happy for him, another part sad.

It was more changes to deal with at a time when her whole world was in flux. She wasn't sure she was up for it but then again, this was not about her. It was all about her best friend Kirby and his new adventure. She needed to support him like he supported her. Always and forever.

"Yes," said Kirby enthusiastically, pulling her out of her rather selfish thoughts. "And I am asking for a favor. I really want you to watch me, if you don't mind. To make sure everything goes okay."

"Of course I will. I'd be honored and thank you for asking me. Are you nervous?"

"Yes. The queen said it's normal to feel this way because it's something new. But mostly I am ready. It is time. It will be my fifth and final shedding and to be honest, I'm more thrilled than anything. To emerge as a butterfly is my dream in life. The ultimate goal. And it's finally going to happen."

Jenna reached over to give him a hug.

"I'm here for you, Kirby. In every way. Is it happening right now?"

"Yes. Right now."

She hugged him again, probably for the last time in his caterpillar form, then she watched as he climbed up to the ceiling and crawled out onto a branch.

He looked back at her, waved, and she blew him a kiss.

Then he got to work.

First, he spun a silken mat and hooked himself to it, hanging upside down. Total fascination took over as she observed him wiggle and shake repeatedly, going about the task of creating a nesting area, his very own blue/green chrysalis with golden dots of color sprinkled here and there. The finished product, seemingly a lot of work, was a complete masterpiece. He had completed another stage in his development and new life awaited when he was ready. Jenna was thrilled for him.

"I'm here for you, Kirby," she cried. "Don't you worry. I will watch you until you emerge again in all your glory."

All was quiet.

She missed him already. A lot.

Gone was the caterpillar who had been her pillar of strength, her rock, and best friend at the Manor. He had stayed by her side throughout her stay...

Enough about her.

Now it was time to repay Kirby's kindness by being *his* rock. He had given so much to her; she really wanted to give so much back to him. He deserved to be taken care of, in total love, the way he had taken care of her. She was never leaving him.

She sat down to watch...day and night...night and day...

Shelly brought her food periodically, even encouraged her to join them at the table, but no way could she do that. She took her promise to care for Kirby seriously. After all, he had asked her to be there with him and she was determined to be present the second he broke through his chrysalis. She wanted him to know she was keeping her promise.

And along with the wait, came an unexpected bonus.

Surprisingly, Kirby's journey also became her own personal voyage along with him. His growth not only amazed her but also seemed to change her.

As time ticked by, she imagined herself in her own cocoon, continually and figuratively shedding her own skin and becoming increasingly more aware, alert, and living moment by moment, day by day. As she watched Kirby carefully, noticing every nuance of his new growth inside his safe place, she slowly began to witness the beautiful butterfly he was turning into. His chrysalis became increasingly transparent and she could already see his new shape, his gorgeous wings, the white dots on his body. She felt she was also evolving, symbolically turning into a butterfly too, albeit a human one, step by step, practicing all she had learned, and beginning to love this freer, happier Jenna. The one who was no longer muddled all the time and was beginning to experience joy in life again. She loved feeling like the little child she once was, when life was exciting, safe, joyful and when jumping through mud puddles, building leaf forts and creating snowmen were special occasions and laughter was a constant.

Her haunting question surfaced from time to time.

Did she feel ready to go home yet? To be back with her family?

Each time it arose, she searched her heart.

Not yet.

But soon.

She could feel a readiness emerging. A restlessness. A desire to be with her children and husband with renewed love, strength and wisdom.

Hopefully in the near future.

"Hello, my dear."

Immersed in her thoughts, she was startled. She looked towards the door to see who it was.

"Oh, hello, Queen."

"Are you still watching Kirby?"

"Yes, I am. It's any time now."

"Yes, it is. Do you want me to stay a while, so you can get some sleep? I'll wake you up when he starts to emerge. I know you want to be here for that, for sure."

"Oh no. I'm okay. I made a promise to stay and I want to honor Kirby's wishes. I'm so excited for him. But I also really do miss him so."

"Just curious. Do you think your family might miss you? Like you miss Kirby?"

"Nah." She shook her head. "Well, maybe. Or at least miss my driving them places. I really wish they would but I kind of doubt it, though. I wasn't much of a mother. I'm also still not wanting to be home yet. I do miss them, but I find I'm getting better here and maybe soon I'll long to go. But only when I'm ready, as you always say."

"What was your family like? With your own parents? Are they still alive?"

"No, neither of them."

Silence.

"Well, I guess they were just like me," Jenna finally answered. "Busy. Or at least my mother was. When I was really young, things seemed pretty okay and I have some good memories. But then my dad got sick with a lot of ailments, couldn't work, and Mom took care of him, all the time, while still working full time at a bank. She was the major bread winner.”

“How did you feel?”

“Well, I knew my mom had a lot on her plate, so I tried to help out the best I could.”

“But how did you *feel*?”

Funny how she had never thought of that. Her feelings never seemed overly important.

“Ummmm…” A tear dripped down. “I missed her a lot. I didn’t see much of her between her work and caring for my dad. I felt neglected, upset, scared, frightened. Basically all alone. There were no more trips to the park or the museum or the beach. Not only that, my dad became very critical of me. It was as if he took his anger over not being able to work out on me. I did nothing right in his eyes. He used to call me Jittery Jenna because I was so nervous around him, I would drop things, trip over things. He never figured out that his constant derision made me like that.”

The butterfly kept quiet.

“It was not the greatest upbringing, but I can’t blame my folks for how I am today. I’m an adult. I should know better.”

“It’s not blaming, little one. It’s learning, growing and healing.”

“Well, if I’m honest, guess I am doing the same to my own kids,” said Jenna, sighing. “Never thought of that. Unfortunately, seems like I never learned anything, just continued on like my parents. My mother used to tell me to pray lots, but was so caught up in worry and work that I’m sure she didn’t follow her own advice. Prayer never seemed to work for her, so I dismissed it. I just kept quiet, never telling her stuff, keeping everything inside. And I began to avoid my dad and tune out his constant critiques. Honestly, I really am doing the same to my kids, aren’t I? I’m busy all the time, criticizing everyone and tuning them right out. I’m a really awful person.”

“I’m not here to judge you, Jenna. Just wanting the best for you. Wanting you to learn, and grow, and wishing you could stop berating yourself.”

"I do appreciate this and I also know you've been through a lot, too. It helps me knowing that, because you bring me much hope that I really can change."

"As I've mentioned before, it's usually when we are faced with crises that we evolve, or at least are more willing to change, realizing the way we lived before was making us unhappy and simply just not working."

"So basically everyone here has had some sort of turning point that led them to change direction in life?"

"Correct."

"Well, getting fired was my undoing. All the sacrifices and it came to nothing. I really wanted to step off the busy train and noticing Kirby on my deck, which brought back my love of nature, somehow really affected me."

"Well it brought you here and you seem to be healing and happier, so it really wasn't all for naught."

"You're right. I am also seeing my family with new eyes and discovering ways I want to change how I've been dealing with them. First of all, I need to start really seeing them and listen and love them for who they are, not as I want them to be, or imagine them to be."

"Good. Now tell me about law. After all, it sounds like you really do love being a lawyer. Is that true?"

Jenna could almost feel her eyes shine.

"Yes, I do love it, and I can still remember one of the first cases I handled. It was a young teenage boy who was accused of stealing a large sum of money at work. In the end, I was able to uncover the fact that he never took it at all. The very manager who accused him was the one doing the stealing. I managed to save this boy from possible imprisonment and a permanent black mark on his record."

"How wonderful that you were able to help. You really made a difference in that teenager's life."

"Yes, I felt I did. I love taking cases where I believe in my client's truth. I often do pro bono work as well, to help the underdog who can't afford the hiring of a lawyer. I wouldn't be surprised if that is why my bosses' son wanted to get rid of me. From what I gather, he seems all about making money, not helping others at all."

"So you enjoy being a lawyer. You know that for sure."

"Yes, but..." Jenna's face clouded over. "I think I'm missing something in the world of law."

"And what would that be?"

"Well, being here and out and about with Kirby has reminded me of how much I have always loved nature in all its glory. At one time I thought I would get into environmental law and devote myself to saving our earth."

"Can you do both?"

"Um, I'm not sure. Maybe. I'd like that and it's certainly something to think about. And pray about."

"Yes, it is. It is important to open our hearts to ways we may use our gifts. What about the wife and mother role? Is it one you want?"

Jenna was aware she usually talked about being a lawyer in more glowing terms than when she talked about her family. Probably because she had more success at work than at home. When it came to her family life, she really was a failure.

The faces of her husband and children walked across a stage cemented in her mind. Her heart lurched. She really did miss them.

"Yes, it is what I want. But in truth, I'm better at law then being a wife and mom. For some reason I am really lousy at family life. I used to be close to my husband, now not so much. And obviously I'm not close to my children one bit."

"Being a mother, as well as a wife, can be hard work at times."

"Yes, and I'm so bad at it. Problems appear right in front of my nose and I don't notice. I seem to just dwell in my busy world, not aware of reality in most cases."

"I know you love them though. I can see it in your eyes when you talk about them."

"I do. But it's not enough."

"Yes, it is, little one. Real love *is* enough. I love every caterpillar here, but real love involves loving yourself first, really seeing yourself for who you are and healing the painful parts, which will enable you to love and see others more clearly. It all takes time."

"I certainly hope I can be like you. You're amazing."

She laughed. "Not at all and certainly not always. As I've mentioned before, it takes time, focus and patience."

"So you think my family might still love me?"

"Yes. I know so. You just need to discover the real truth about life."

"And what again is the truth? I can't seem to get it."

The queen smiled one of her huge beams that lit up the room.

"I know I sound repetitive but love really is the truth. Love is what it's all about. And look. I think someone else is trying to tell you the same thing."

Kirby's chrysalis was gently swaying.

Jenna jumped up.

"Really? Kirby looks even more ready, right? Do you think it will be soon? Maybe even now?"

"Yes. I think it's going to happen fast."

Leave it to Kirby to sense when she was confused and choose that exact time to emerge to comfort her, as well as drive home the love point.

She grabbed the ladder and climbed up, sticking to her promise to keep an eye on him.

More movement on Kirby's part.

He was about to break free. It was really going to happen.

Tears streamed down her face as he appeared, slowly at first, then a bit quicker.

Jenna crossed her fingers, hoping he'd be fine, until all of a sudden she wanted to scream with joy, because he was all out, wet wings and all. He clasped onto his cocoon and immediately turned to look at her.

His eyes were a shimmery blue, glowing with excitement and Jenna's heart exploded with love. It seemed as if a new chrysalis of extraordinary peace enveloped him, a sense of serenity and joy that reached out to her as well. He was free. Totally free. And it was a blessing to have witnessed his transformation.

A total miracle.

Jenna stayed nearby as he rested, gathering strength. She noted how she had to fight her own instincts to try to fix him, make it better, dry his wings for him. But she knew it certainly wasn't what he needed. He could do all that himself. So she simply watched. If he wanted help, she'd be there.

Finally, after a while, he flapped his wings and pushed off, immediately flying over to land right beside her. Jenna climbed down the ladder and he leaned in to give her a soft kiss.

"Hello, Miss Jenna."

"Oh hello, Kirby. I'm so happy to see you. Are you really okay?"

"Yes, I am. I am more than okay. I am ecstatic. Thank you for keeping watch. I saw you there day and night and I really appreciated it."

"It was my honor to do so. Oh, Kirby, I am so thrilled for you. And you still have your gorgeous blue eyes."

"Yeah? Pretty great, huh. It will happen to you one day, too. Just you wait."

"Do you really think so?"

"Yes, I do. It's already happening."

"Thank you for believing in me."

"Always. And now, Miss Jenna." His eyes twinkled. "May I have this dance?"

Our happy dance. Of course. He hadn't forgotten.

"You bet. I'd be honored."

We twisted and twirled and jumped and boogied. If the king and queen thought it was odd seeing a tiny human and a big butterfly dance together, they never said a word. They simply watched, huge smiles on their faces.

Jenna especially loved when Kirby spread his gorgeous wings, trying them out, moving with ease, barely containing the thrill in his eyes.

They finally stopped, with Kirby's wings gently wrapped around her. She held on tight, basking in his love.

"I think we've perfected this," he whispered.

"You got that right."

He finally pulled away, his wings starting to flutter. "I need to go now," he said.

"Yes, it's time. Time for you to fly. Will you come back and visit?"

"Yes. It's a promise."

And with that, he whispered something in her ear, then flew up and out into the world.

And Jenna was sad again.

That was, until she felt the warmth of the queen standing beside her.

"He is happy, my friend. And one day you will be too."

She sure hoped so.

"Guess what his final words were, Queen?"

"Oh, please tell me."

"He said that love is not only the answer, but also the question."

"Wise words."

"Yes," Jenna said. "He knew I would get it."

"And what did you get?"

"Well, when we question our life's purpose, it is important to ask *who are we called to love*? The answer should always be *God, ourselves, and others as ourselves*."

"True," said the queen. "The question and the answer. Kirby knows the real truth about life and love."

Jenna smiled.

She was growing closer to learning the truth, too.

She felt it in her heart.

Living it was a whole other matter.

Eleven

Jenna stretched out on the grass and stared up at the sky.

"You are so beautiful," she whispered in awe, delighting in its brilliant shades of blue, highlighting the white fluffy clouds drifting across, almost as if in slow motion. Breathtaking, always.

Lately she had taken to going out for short walks and falling completely in love all over again and again with nature and its beauty. Yes, she even had a new appreciation for spiders. It was as if everything spoke to her and it was a happy, delightful conversation. She enjoyed lying in the grass and really observing, as if for the very first time, gorgeous sunrises and sunsets, in all its pinks, golds, blues and oranges. She loved to experience the sun, wind and rain on her cheeks, noticing the colors and various hues of the green grass where she walked, as well as all the flowers and plants she feasted her eyes on. She was reaching out to embrace life with open arms, meditating daily and beginning to live more in the present where she was practicing seeing herself and all the caterpillars and butterflies as they really were. Slowly, she was continuing to view life as it was. Not as she willed it to be, expected it to be, or felt disillusioned by how it appeared. She accepted it all and learned to roll with it.

She was ultimately striving to be her authentic self, the best she could be, in every possible way, always in acceptance of moments of joy, sadness, and all the many ways she experienced life.

But...

The eternal question rang out again, as if accompanied with drums and cymbals. The same question she asked herself each and every single day.

Was it time to go home?

Jenna closed her eyes. She thought of Ellie, Jason and her husband Scott. She longed to see them but something still held her back.

Her eyes popped open.

No, she was still not ready.

She didn't have that 'go' feeling that would send her back fast. It was not depression this time. Not feeling sorry for herself or wallowing in self-pity. Not feeling her family was better off without her. Just a strong sense of not being ready. A feeling there was still more to learn. The queen said she would know when it was time and she counted on those words of wisdom. One day it would happen. Even sooner than she thought. She was sure of it.

So she continued her stay at Milkweed Manor.

She extended the many days of self-searching, figuring things out or going with the flow, letting go of old worn-out worries and fears and clearing her head. And lots and lots of healing.

It was not easy, though.

It was hard to change a lifetime of habits and required a lot of patience. Slowly, ever so slowly, with tiny baby steps, she was beginning to be alert to when future and past thoughts took over, obscuring her present moment. She would then take action by figuratively stepping back and allowing thoughts to surface, taking note, but not letting them control her. The healing process allowed her feelings of hurt, anger and sadness to drift away so her focus could be solidly on the moment, which was really all anyone had at any given time. She realized that.

And she was doing it.

Bit by bit.

And miracle of miracles, she was continuing to lose weight, which absolutely stunned her.

The butterflies were right.

Love really was the answer.

Simple but profound.

By learning to love herself, or at least trying hard to do so, it certainly did become easier to refuse to put junk food into her body and she even threw out the chocolate bars and cookies she'd brought back from home. She had never realized that she had quite the addiction to food and stuffing herself put her in basically a stupor, thrusting her on a merry-go-round of hate. Now she loved feeling physically better by choosing foods that nourished her and she also was increasingly more relaxed. She didn't need her addiction nor want it anymore. She was trusting herself instead, and doing what made her feel good. It was not about the food anymore, but all about what made her happy and contributed to her journey of becoming her real self.

It was a lot to take in.

And she really missed Kirby.

Dearly.

He had been a huge support system for her. It was different than with the queen. He was quieter and it was his calm, solid presence that touched her heart, whereas the queen challenged her with questions and insights that revealed deep truths. She had also enjoyed her jaunts through nature with Kirby, and not only that, she missed his humor and optimistic view of life.

And his dancing.

She always looked around for him, hoping to catch a glimpse. But no such luck. Guess he was so much in love with his new world he'd forgotten her. But she really didn't blame him one bit. Soaring into the skies sure looked like the best way to live.

"Well, time to get ready for the day," Jenna said, getting up from the grass and brushing herself off. "Bye sky, bye flowers, bye plants, bye all creatures. See ya later." She grinned at her silliness, but they had all become her close friends. Nature sure was healing her as well and for this she was eternally grateful. It was all a real blessing being here at the Manor. The best ever.

"Well, hello, Miss Jenna."

Startled, she turned to find a large butterfly hovering right behind her. She stared into its eyes and her heart skipped a beat.

"Kirby. Is this really you?" His use of Miss gave it away, not to mention the blue eyes, but she wanted to be sure.

"Yes, it is." He smiled, landing beside her.

Jenna threw herself into his arms, or wings, so to speak.

"This is my lucky day. Oh, I'm so glad to see you. You must have read my mind, because I was just thinking about you and hey, you remembered. You came back to see me."

"Yes, I did. A promise is a promise." He pulled back. "How are you doing?"

"Oh so much better."

"I can tell. You are glowing."

"Really? You can?"

"Yes. I've been keeping an eye on you, and the queen has been updating me in terms of your progress. I hear you're growing tremendously."

"You actually heard that?"

"Yes. So I felt it was time to come back for a visit." He smiled. "And here I find you out enjoying nature. I'm so proud of you."

"Loving it, loving everything, and it's all because of you. All those rides we took and watching you embrace the sun, the moon, the grass, the trees... oh how I have missed you so much. But seeing you before me, in all your glory, astounds me. Emerging as a butterfly certainly agrees with you."

"Sure does. I love and embrace my new life."

"I'm so happy to hear that. But you know, Kirby, lying around thinking about you has me curious. I'm ashamed to admit that I've been so wrapped up in my own problems, I never asked you what *your* story was. How you ended up at Milkweed Manor. Am I being too nosy to ask now? How your own personal journey led to such peace?"

"I'll always answer your questions, Miss Jenna. Come, sit with me a while."

And she did, curled up beside him, wrapped in the comfort of his wings.

"Here's what happened to me. The leaf sheltering my egg, was torn off somehow, presumably by a wild animal, and I was born far away from my home. After hatching and eating my shell and the leaf, I had nowhere else to go. I was scared and confused."

"Oh no, poor Kirby."

"And poor Kirby was how I felt. I wandered around looking for my home and discovered I had another problem."

"Yes? What was it?"

"I had blue eyes. And no one else did."

"But they're beautiful."

"Well, that's what you think. However, I was different and everyone else was suspicious of me. I was shunned, ignored, avoided so much that one day I just curled up, wanting to die. I felt lost, abandoned and had no hope whatsoever. I was all alone in the world. Or so I thought."

Tears flowed down Jenna's face.

"Wish I could have been there for you."

He smiled. "That would have been nice."

"So what happened next?"

"Somehow I managed to pull myself together, summon up some courage, and decided to look for my home one last time. I walked and walked but still got nowhere. Eventually, I sat down again, this time praying for help. And guess what?"

"What?"

"Little did I know that the queen somehow saw my struggles, picked me up and brought me to Milkweed Manor. The answer to my prayer."

"She did?"

Come to think of it.

When Jenna was alone on that deck, she had looked for God too, asking for help. Maybe that was the very first step. A last resort prayer, the willingness to ask for guidance, to believe it really might happen. Also, the openness and readiness to accept it.

Whew! She was glad she'd prayed and also was open to answers. Milkweed Manor had truly been her Godsend. Sounded like it was the same for Kirby.

Listen. He was speaking again.

"Yes, the queen became my guide. I was still quite a mess, sad and disillusioned. I basically did what you did. Calmed down, stepped back, observed, healed, and slowly became my authentic self, nestled in peace. With direction, of course."

"And now here you are. A beacon of light, hope and love."

"Well, thank you."

"No, thank *you*. You inspire me, especially since I am trying to do the same thing."

"I'm happy to do so. As well, you inspire me also with your tenacity and commitment to being the best that you can be. But hey, does this answer your question?"

"Sure does. Thank you for sharing."

"No problem. Anything for you. So now, enough about me, would you like to go for a ride?"

"A ride? Are you kidding? I'd love to."

"Good. I've already cleared it with Shelly and the queen. You are off kitchen and chrysalis duty for a while and you are free to go." He turned around and said, "So, hop on."

And she did, feeling right at home with her mentor, anticipating a ride she'd never forget.

Up they went, high into the sky where Kirby whirled and twirled, twisted and turned. It was like a new dance, this time in the air. At times she felt afraid when she viewed how far away from the earth they were, but she quickly relaxed, trusting her friend, and allowing herself to enjoy the moment, and the view.

Her joy heightened as time went on, until she was ready to burst.

Finally, not able to keep it to herself any longer, Jenna screamed, "I'm flying. I'm actually flying. Wheeee..."

It felt so wonderful. So freeing. So utterly fantastic.

"Great. But are you really doing all right?" asked Kirby. "You're not scared, are you?"

"Not one bit. At least not any more. I'm loving this."

"Good."

She looked around, thoroughly enjoyed the scenery, the bright colorful gardens below, the parks where families gathered and laughed with joy, and the puffy clouds they seemed to sail right on through. She was sure he was trying to show her the joy of land and sky and she loved every minute of it.

Finally, Kirby flew around a large building and descended onto a windowsill.

Jenna knew exactly where she was. She should have known it would not be just a casual ride. Things were mighty deep at the Manor, full of experiences and wisdom to learn.

She peered into the window.

Her husband was sitting at his desk, in his office, at his school.

She gazed at him hungrily, stunned at the longing that swarmed her.

I miss him, she thought. *I really do miss him.*

"Oh, Kirby. You did this on purpose, didn't you?" She turned to watch his expression.

"Well, not really." His eyes twinkled. "I follow my gut and do what I feel I should do. I don't know the end results."

"It still reminds me of that Scrooge movie where I'm observing my past life. This time not at my house but at my husband's workplace."

"Yes, you're right, it is a bit similar to the movie. Guess it's making you re-look at your life."

"Sure does. And the results aren't pretty but I do learn so much from these interludes. Mostly painful stuff but things I need to face. Wonder what I'll discover today."

She looked back in the window and watched as Scott kept repeatedly brushing his hair off his face, the way he did when he was nervous. His eyes looked haunted, worried, upset.

"Is something wrong with him?" she asked.

"You'll see," said Kirby.

She saw her husband hit numbers on his cell phone, then lift it to his ear.

Was that a tear drifting down his cheek? Really?

"Mr. Allen, this is Principal Evans. I was wondering how Stewart is? Is he okay? Will he pull through?"

Jenna turned towards Kirby. "Who is Stewart?"

"A student who overdosed," said Kirby. "Right here at school. Your husband did CPR on him. He is speaking to the boy's father at the moment."

"Oh, how awful. So you've been keeping an eye on Scott, too?"

"I have," he said.

"Thank you."

Nice to know her husband was under surveillance, at least until she made it back home to take over the job. If ever that was.

She continued to watch as her husband hung up, put his head down on his arms resting on his desk, and sobbed.

She was shocked. She had only seen him cry one time before and that was on their wedding day. Tears of joy, that is.

"Did Stewart live?"

"Yes," said Kirby. "It was touch and go, but yes, he did. Thanks to your husband's quick actions."

Amazing that Kirby knew all this. The magic of the Manor, for sure. Jenna had come to just accept it.

"Oh, thank goodness." But she was still unnerved at how upset her husband was, which was a reminder about the serious nature of his job that somehow she had forgotten.

Jenna knew as the principal of a busy high school, Scott dealt with extremely dire situations, but he never brought issues home with him or talked about them. Mostly because they were in confidence, so he was not able to discuss them freely, but still, he needed support to see him through these hard times. Guess she had just thrown his work stress and possible heart-break all out of her mind, and stayed wrapped up in her own concerns. Guess she had never extended kindness to him, gentleness, or compassion for all *he* went through. Or at least in quite some time.

And here he was crying, moved, upset, yet no doubt thrilled the student had lived.

Her heart went out to him.

He was her rock, like Kirby was, only she realized she hadn't given anything back.

Sigh.

Once again, here was another person she wasn't there for.

Memories took hold.

She had met her husband at a soup kitchen. Concerned with the plight of the homeless, they had joined a small army of volunteers united to help raise money to at least be able to offer a warm meal to everyone in need. Jenna had always worked there on Fridays, so did Scott. Friendship ensued, and soon they had fallen in love and were inseparable. They used to spend many long hours discussing every moment of their days and delighted in each other's company.

Sigh - again.

They had so many dreams back then. She wanted to help people through law while Scott felt called to minister to teenagers through education. They also wanted children but it sure seemed as if all their love and joy had gotten lost in raising children, pressures, his busy job and her aspirations to make partner. Yes, they were doing good work, she as a lawyer, he as a principal, but their marriage was suffering, not to mention how it filtered down to their children. Instead of enjoying what they had achieved, they were stressed out by it all and had sure made a mess of things. Or at least she had. Big time.

She glanced at Kirby.

"Thank you. I needed to see this. To face the truth."

"Yes, I think so too."

"I believe I really need to be alone right now. To think. Would you mind?"

"No, not at all. I understand after you experience a revelation, you seek alone time. I'll take you back to the Manor."

"No, please. There is somewhere else I'd like to go."

"Sure. Just name it."

"My deck," burst out Jenna. "Hate to bother you, but I really want to go back to my deck."

To where this journey once began.

Twelve

"For good?" asked Kirby, looking surprised. "Is it time to go home?"

"No, not yet. Soon, though. Right now, I'd just like to stay there a while to reflect and then go see the queen. Would that be okay?"

"Certainly, whatever you need. I'll leave you there for as long as you want, then bring you back to the Manor when you're ready."

"Okay. Thank you, Kirby. That would be terrific. You're so kind."

"I just want the best for you, Miss Jenna, and I'll help in any way."

"Thank you."

He flew to her house, circled a few times, then slowly lowered her down onto the deck.

"I'll keep watch from above," he said. "Just beckon when you are finished here."

"Thank you, I will."

Jenna stood on the deck for a while, reliving the moment she first saw Kirby. It also was the first time she'd prayed since about forever. Who knew those encounters, moments when she reached out, would have changed her world so dramatically?

Best thing ever, she thought.

Next, she walked over to the deck door and, still being small, searched for the tiny crack, the very one she crawled through with Kirby a few times.

"There it is."

Stretching up on her toes, she managed to pop through it and hurried down the hall to the kitchen.

Good. Ellie and Jason were sitting at the table, both engaged in what looked like homework. This time she wanted to see them. In secret, of course.

Now, how to get up on the counter so she could be near them without being discovered?

She looked around.

Hmmmm... the garbage can.

Maybe she could climb up on it and then, with some fancy footwork, reach the countertop.

Panting, determined, and rejoicing that she was much more agile and definitely stronger than she used to be, she managed to get up on top of the can. It was similar to rock climbing, for she had scaled the aluminum siding, clinging to the ridges that popped out of the design. Once on top, she was able to grab hold of the handle of a drawer and swing herself up and onto the counter.

Plop.

Amazing. She had made it.

Hiding behind her usual spot, the toaster, with just her head popped out, she looked at her children.

Really looked.

Her heart flooded with joy at the simple pleasure of just watching them, savoring them, aching for them.

But she did note that Jason still looked a mess with his tangled too long hair and ill-fitting clothes. Ellie appeared even thinner. They also seemed worried, tired, with eyes too old for their ages. They were young, they should be enjoying life. But they didn't seem to. Not one bit.

Such an awful shame.

And it reminded her of her own childhood. She had to grow up too fast back then, with an ill, critical father and a demanding, worried mother.

Darn it.

Once again she thought about how history was repeating itself in her very own kitchen. A room she had once decorated with love and anticipated years of happy meals and swapping exciting stories.

"I hear a car," said Ellie, jumping into Jenna's thoughts. "I think Mom's home."

Sadly, Jenna watched them pack up their books and practically run upstairs. It was obvious they avoided her. Why, she wasn't sure. Did she question them too much? Was she too nosy? Did she only talk about how stressed *her* day was? Was she crabby? A total pain and hard to be around?

Sigh. She was probably all of the above.

That was why she never knew they did assignments at the table.

Was she that much of a drag her own kids dodged her? Tried to stay away?

Guess so.

Then again, she did the very same, every time she refused to take their phone calls at work and answered her cell at suppertime.

She ignored them.

And the truth hurt. All over again.

A door slammed, and in walked her husband, home from work.

She peered at him, this time noticing his face that was once smooth and supple, now had wrinkles lining his forehead, and he appeared exhausted, worn-out, lifeless.

No one was happy here.

That was a given.

No one.

For at least what seemed a long, long while.

Figuratively, she stepped back from her mind, and paid attention.

How was she feeling?

Kirby's ride has sure evoked a lot of emotion and sent streamers of longing shooting through her. Important to note—longing not self-loathing for a change.

She closed her eyes.

Images of Scott, Jason and Ellie walked across her heart and formed a colorful collage of good memories.

Like the time Scott cooked dinner for her at his apartment, proposed on bended knee, proclaiming forever love, reached for the ring to give her and embarrassed as anything, discovered he'd left it at home. He quickly opened a cupboard door, grabbed a piece of string and wrapped it around her finger. Peals of laughter ensued, as he picked her up and swung her around in his arms. Filled with joy, they were so much in love and anticipated a happy marriage.

She remembered the first time Ellie called her 'Mama' and how honored she'd felt gazing into her daughter's vulnerable eyes, vowing to always earn the overwhelming trust she saw there.

She even summoned up Jason's excitement the time they'd built a snowman in the yard and he'd pulled off his own scarf and wrapped it around the iceman's neck, calling him Da Da number two. Scott being his number one always.

Laughter, long walks, hot chocolate, baking cookies, lots of hugs and joy, pure joy, was what their family life had been about.

Where had it all gone?

Guess it had dwindled away as fear took hold.

Then there was the stress of taking on a fulltime job, trying to make a dream come true. Not to forget the long hours, the running the children around to their appointments, the hasty meals, the conversation that was always rushed and unsatisfying.

Come to think of it, it really wasn't her job that was the issue, if she were really honest. It was mixing up her priorities. The desire to be made partner became more important than her family, as she continually got lost in deadlines, paperwork, clients, unhappiness, sadness.

Pain sliced through her.

Hurt and frustration joined in, along with huge guilt for not being there for her husband and children as time marched on.

She felt ashamed.

Go deeper, she thought. *Search your heart. Breathe. In and out. In and out.*

How do you really feel now?

And then it happened.

Like a breathtaking glorious rainbow after a particularly harsh storm, Jenna's love for her family burst forth in all its many hues of color.

The truth emerged, finally.

She truly did love them and missed them with all her heart.

Love, the most important element in life, was there. Real love, good love, forever love.

She longed to touch their faces, hug them, listen to what they had to say but most important, be a part of their lives again.

Yes, she had failed in her roles as wife and mother. But she wanted another chance.

Could she redeem herself?

Could she start again?

Or were they better off without her?

Opening her eyes, she stood tall.

She knew what she had to do.

She had made her decision.

She needed to know.

She wanted to see if all she had learned, rooted in the Manor, could be transferred to her real life in the so-called real world.

Could it?

Would it?

She *had* to try. To 'see.'

Jenna waited until her husband went upstairs, probably to change into more comfortable clothes, and slid down from the counter, onto the garbage can and white-knuckled it back to the floor. After making it out on the deck again, she looked up, saw Kirby flying nearby and waved him down.

He landed beside her and she quickly hopped on.

"Thank you for waiting, my friend. I would really like to talk to the queen now."

"A great idea."

Jenna loved how he asked no questions. He somehow just seemed to know her heart, her needs. He never pushed but always made sure he was on her side. Once again she thought, she was lucky to know him.

Quickly flying back, he landed at the Manor.

"I'll see you soon," he said, wrapping his wings around her in a warm embrace.

She held on tight, not wanting to let him go.

Finally, she pulled back.

"Promise?" she asked.

"Promise."

"And thank you for being just about the best friend ever."

"Remember, it was not just one way," he said. "You were there for me too, especially when I really needed you. Now, go on. I believe the queen will be waiting for you. It's good news, right? I can see it on your face."

"Right."

After one more hug, and a sassy, mischievous wink, he soared into the skies. Jenna watched him, her heart full of love for this kind, gentle creature who taught her so much just by being his authentic self. She was one lucky person.

Waving until she could no longer see him, she turned around and headed to the Monarch's chambers.

She knocked at the entrance.

Thirteen

"Yes, dear?" asked the queen, arriving in the doorway.

"So very sorry to bother you, but may I talk to you?"

"Of course. Any time. Come on in."

"Thank you."

She walked in and looked around. She had never been there and was charmed by the eclectic feel of the room. Everything, from the vase of cut wildflowers mixed with dandelions, collections of brightly colored stones, to the charming wooden sculptures scattered throughout, was unique, soothing, comforting and pleasing to the eye. She immediately relaxed.

"Your room is beautiful," said Jenna.

"Thank you. I only allow pieces that bring me joy to enter this room and I put them in places where I can relish them. Those sculptures, by the way, were created by Kirby."

"Really? I knew he fashioned amazing furniture, but these statues are stunning." She looked closely at each one. "I see they all depict either a tree or an animal."

"Yes, all the things I love."

"So, I get it. You have beautifully created a nest. A place of refuge, peace, loveliness."

"Exactly. I don't care if anything matches in terms of color or placement as long as they come together in my heart."

"Another point to learn. To build an environment restful to the soul. A place to ground myself."

"Yes. Having a space to nurture and nourish your authentic self, really helps create peace."

"You're right. I feel it here. I did once take great care over my house, trying to create spaces of love, but of course, promptly forgot to continue with this. Then again, it really wasn't a comfortable nest because I was focused more on being stylish. But walking in here really made me feel good, so I'll have to remember this and revamp my home."

The queen smiled. "You are a terrific house guest, Jenna, so eager to learn and grow. Now please, sit. I take it, judging by the excitement in your eyes and voice, you have something to talk to me about?"

"I do."

Jenna settled herself on a small stool and leaned forward, barely containing her enthusiasm.

"I believe it is time to go home."

"Yes?"

"Yes."

"Please tell me about it."

"Well, I think I have learned many lessons here. Wisdom that will help me when I am back with my family. I'm ready to try."

"Good. I believe you have, too. So just what have you gleaned here? Maybe it will help to put it into words."

"Thank you. Yes, it would." Jenna leaned back, paused for a moment as she collected her thoughts, then said, "Well, I am praying now, something I haven't done in years. I have also learned and practiced to step back and observe how I feel, my reactions, my fears, joys and concerns. By doing this, my feelings no longer overpower or control me and I don't get caught up in them. I simply learn from them. I also see the many ways I need healing and I have asked for God's help in these areas, especially with deep-rooted ancient thoughts stemming from my childhood. This helps me calm down and

I no longer twist and turn with endless old beliefs and mind games. I am also learning to not worry about my future and live each moment as it comes."

Speaking of calming herself, she took a deep breath and let it out.

Again.

In and out.

"I feel I have been transformed, Queen. Slowly become enlightened, even. Oh, not completely, of course. I believe it is a lifelong commitment to strive to live as my authentic self. But being here at Milkweed Manor was like my very own chrysalis where I shed many layers of pain. It has been therapeutic seeing myself, my children and husband in a new light. It is time. Time to be with them. I feel ready. Ready to love them."

"And what is love to you?"

"A loaded question, for sure. Not sure I have exact answers for I'm still learning, but well, it is many things, I guess. It is belonging and feeling part of a greater good. Some call it God but like you say whenever we pray at meal times, many call it different things, a higher power, a source, nature and so on. In my world I do call it God. It is feeling love, loving God, loving myself, loving others as they are. It is not being caught up in anxiety and allowing worries, fears and trying to be good enough, trying to please others, to cloud my days. It is living in the present, for at any given second the present is all we really have. I keep reminding myself of this daily."

"You're growing closer," said the queen. "Evolving. And you are wise to know that this is a lifetime commitment. A desire to grow and change forever."

"Definitely. I can see that but ohhhhh, Queen, I will miss everyone here, but I so long to be with my family again and really *see* their smiles, their laughter, their joys and moments of fear and doubt. To care for them with all my heart."

The queen smiled. "Yes, there is incredible delight seeing people for who they are and not through the misty, shadowy eyes of worry."

"But right now there seems to be so much pain in my family and I'm wondering. How do I fix it? How do I get others to change? When do I speak up or remain silent?"

"You don't try to fix things, Jenna. You just keep on being yourself, growing, becoming authentic, living in the present and only then will you know when to speak up or remain quiet. Maybe others will be influenced. Maybe not. But you keep on being you. Never forget that."

"Keep on being me. Great advice and hopefully in time I will no longer try to fix others, realizing taking care of myself is the best place to start. And another question."

"Yes?"

"Here in Milkweed Manor, I feel safe. I am surrounded by people committed to growing, to being their real selves, to being the best they can be. Out in my world, I will be around people who can be negative, unsupportive, not in tune with living this way. Toxic, actually. How do I deal with them?"

"A very wise question."

"So what do I do?"

"Well, as always, as I mentioned before, you remain living in your own authenticity always and in the present moment. You don't react to others' negativity, or become like them again. The more secure you feel, grounded in love, you will have compassion for them, knowing they are struggling too. And, if you have to, you walk away. It will no doubt be a great challenge but you can do it."

"You think so?"

"I know so. You be you, the real you, that is all that is necessary. All action or inaction, comes out of this."

Easily said, thought Jenna, difficult to do. But she had been trying hard to allow her inner self to be set free and felt in time it would get easier.

"Er, Queen, do *you* think I'm ready?"

"Only you can make that decision."

She was right.

"I think I am."

"Well, Jenna. This is the second time you have said *think*. You still sound doubtful. I wouldn't recommend you go until you are sure. You might be rushing it."

She was absolutely right.

Jenna still sensed doubt deep down in her heart. An unsettling feeling. Something was still not jibing well.

She knew what she had to do.

"Excuse me, Queen. I think I need to go sit in the chrysalis room and reflect. That always seems to set me straight. There is something not quite right about my decision to go home. I'm still feeling a sense of unreadiness."

"A good idea. You need to be sure."

Jenna left and practically ran to her special room. Something really was missing. She wanted to go home, but was still holding back all at the same time.

What was it? What was bothering her?

Sinking down in her chair, she closed her eyes and began breathing in and out again. Big healthy breaths.

In and out.

In and out.

Slowly, ever so slowly, she experienced a deeper peace, one she had never felt.

One she was finally ready for.

During this time of calm, she took note of a great fear she had.

Can people really change?

Had *she* changed?

Or was this just temporary?

Back with her family, would she just sink into old familiar ways and basically stay the same? Living the way she always did?

Was all this learning for naught?

Deep down, this was what was bugging her.

Staying at Milkweed Manor was like going on a vacation, loving it, learning, growing, finally relaxing, and returning home refreshed and vowing never to get stressed out again. Then, after arriving back to all her endless chores, duties, responsibilities, in five minutes going back to the worried, tense woman she always was and nothing changed.

She didn't want to do that ever again. She didn't want to live like that anymore.

She liked the new person she had become, which was really her true self, the self she'd buried over the years, then spent many hours and days uncovering.

How could she stop the old Jenna from happening?

She didn't want to go 'back,' only forward.

More deep breaths. More serenity.

Going deeper... deeper... deeper...

Then suddenly, without forcing it, seeking it, or willing it, a story popped into her mind.

A true story.

About a wonderful person.

A saint, actually.

Saint Paul.

Taught to her by her religion teacher so long ago. Mr. Tilley. She finally remembered his name. And to think she'd felt the class was a waste of time and often daydreamed away the hour of instruction.

Yet here she was, years later, remembering many key passages from the Bible that he had proclaimed in class.

And finally recalling Saint Paul.

She snuggled up deeper into her chair, a smile on her lips, as she reflected on his story, for obviously, without even knowing it, he had left a great impression on her heart. And as her authentic self arose, so did his example.

His life flew through her mind as if playing out on a stage, vivid, exciting, real, mind-boggling.

Forget her mind.

She was looking at him from her eager heart.

For here was a man who disgustingly persecuted followers of Jesus. He hated them, sometimes even making sure they were murdered.

Apparently, as the story went, one day he and several others, were travelling on a road to a city called Damascus. He was out to arrest Christians and put them on trial. Along the way he was embraced by a bright light, so bright he fell to the ground. A voice, claiming to be Jesus, questioned him from the heavens, asking Paul why he persecuted him. Paul was struck blind and spent three days in prayer, eventually emerging, filled with the Holy Spirit, receiving many graces from God, and committed his life to spreading the good news of Jesus Christ. News of peace and love, compassion and kindness... and eternal life.

Wow.

She'd forgotten about Saint Paul until then. She often remembered his words, words of love, but not his story. Guess she'd finally found the space in her being where he resided, bringing her closer to God.

Perfect timing.

Saint Paul was a profound example of a person who had changed. *For good.*

He had been on one path all his life and then, with the grace of God, took another one. He evolved, grew in faith and wisdom, and he touched the world with his reflections.

He reminded her that people really *could* change. They really *could* make a difference.

And for the better.

And it could last. *Forever.*

God bless Mr. Tilley. God bless religion class.

In time she would seek him out and let him know how much he had really taught her.

But most of all.

God bless Saint Paul. And the Holy Spirit that dwelled within. And grace...the grace of God given to us through faith.

All she had learned as well as remembered at the Manor led to a quiet resounding *yes, yes, yes* in her heart.

She knew what the missing ingredient in her life was.

Excited, she opened her eyes and literally ran back to the queen.

"It *is* time," she said, bursting into her room. "I know for sure now. It is time. I know what I was missing."

The queen smiled. "Tell me about it."

"I forgot about the Holy Spirit that dwells in my heart. That Jesus told his disciples that He promised us this, to guide us, to help us, to show us the way," she said excitedly. "I truly believe now that I have been changed for good. For always. By God's grace. I will continue to grow and learn and heal. I realize that I have all the tools I need that will help me back at home. Tools for a lifetime."

"Yes?" asked the queen. "And what are your tools?"

"They are in the words of Saint Paul."

And surprisingly she remembered one of his many powerful messages. Shouldn't be really surprising, though. God seemed to give her exactly what she needed at any given moment.

"He said, *Do not be anxious about anything, but in every situation, by prayer and petition, with thanksgiving, present your requests to God. And the peace of God, which transcends all understanding, will guard your hearts and your minds in Christ Jesus.*"

She paused to let the words sink in, then continued.

"Queen, by the fervent grace of God, this is everything I need to know in life. To pray and give thanks to God and I will receive peace that only comes from God. I will be transformed over and over again by meeting each challenge with faith."

The queen smiled.

"You're glowing," she said. "And radiating peace, harmony, wisdom and joy. Most of all, you have discovered love, real love. I am pleased to say that you, Jenna Evans, have truly become a human butterfly. You have emerged in all your authentic beauty and it is now time for you to soar."

The queen wrapped her wings around her.

"Yes, Jenna, you are finally ready."

Could a smile really grow as big as the moon?

Yes.

Hers just did.

Fourteen

"Her eyes are opening," screamed Ellie. "Oh, Daddy, look, look. Her eyes are opening. She's moving her head. She's looking at us. She's *really* looking at us."

Yes, she was.

Hearing a loud excited voice, Jenna slowly eased out of what seemed to be some kind of stupor. Her husband, son and daughter were staring at her as if they'd never seen her before, eyes wide open, mouths dropped in shock, tears dripping down their cheeks.

Her daughter was still screaming.

"She's awake, she's awake. Daddy, she's awake."

Wait a second.

Panic set in.

What did Ellie mean?

She was awake?

Where was she now?

She moved her head back and forth.

Where were the butterfly curtains? The leaves?

Where was Milkweed Manor?

And the noise. Oh... the noise.

She seemed to be lying in some kind of bed, hooked up to machines beeping shrill and loud and nonstop. It had to be the Manor. Those were the noises she heard there all the time.

She scanned the room again. No, she was somewhere she'd never been.

What was going on?

What had happened?

One minute she was all excited and talking to the queen about going home and the next she was elsewhere. Someplace new. Not the Manor, nor her house. She'd assumed Kirby would fly her back to her deck and somehow, she would magically become a normal size again, enter the kitchen and greet her family. No such luck. She was in another new house or place or... and she was lying down. Not to mention connected to an array of machines for some reason.

She struggled to sit up.

"Where am I?" she asked, noting her voice was raspy, soft, as she tried to keep the panic out of her words, not wanting to upset her children.

"You're safe," said her husband quickly, reaching out to hold her hand. "Hey, take it easy. You fell off the railing on the deck and have a concussion. You've been in a coma for three days, but you're going to be okay."

"Oh."

A coma?

Three days?

No way. She'd been at Milkweed Manor for months and months. Maybe even a year.

What the... ?

She was grateful Scott filled her in on what was going on fast, but he didn't have to lie about it.

Wait!

Was he lying?

Maybe not.

She was going to be okay? Well, at least that was good news.

But a coma?

No way...

But was that the truth?

She had really been in a coma?

Her head flooded with confusion.

Oh, come on.

She had been at the Manor the whole time.

She scanned the room.

Hadn't she?

And wait!

What about the queen, the king, Kirby and Shelly?

Where were they? Did they ever even exist?

Calm yourself, Jenna.

Take deep breaths.

Panic subsided as she took stock.

Surprisingly, she started to giggle, picturing huge caterpillars and butterflies hanging around. They'd freak her family out. They almost freaked *her* out.

Reality became clearer as her head stopped spinning.

So there really was no Milkweed Manor?

She had been right all along? It really was just a dream? A fantasy, driven by a coma? Hallucinations? And all that noise she'd experienced at the Manor was really the machines she was hooked up to?

But she had begun to believe it was all real. She had fallen in love with the Manor so much that she had been thrilled she was there and thoroughly enjoyed the experience.

Movement startled her.

Still giggling about large insects, a monarch suddenly flew towards her and perched on her hand.

She stared at it, marveling at its beauty.

"So weird. That butterfly has been here the whole time," said Jason. "I tried to catch it several times but it kept flying away."

"Yeah," said Ellie. "It's pretty strange. First there was a weird little caterpillar with blue eyes hanging around, then a butterfly. He won't leave your side. It's like he's been watching over you, keeping guard. Just like us."

"And it really is a he," said Scott. "One of the nurses knows about butterflies and she checked. It's a boy due to an extra two dots on his wings. She doesn't know why he has blue eyes, though. Guess it's unique to this one."

A male butterfly. With blue eyes.

Jenna smiled as she stared at the monarch. His compound eyes winked. Instantly, she knew who he was, for in her magical/dream world, butterflies could wink. And she knew one with deep blue sparkly eyes.

"Kirby," she said. "You kept your promise. You're here." She winked back.

Instantly a new wave of peace settled in, enveloping her, relaxing her. Just seeing her best buddy reminded her of all the lessons she had learned at Milkweed Manor, all the wisdom, dream or not. She took another deep cleansing breath and blew it out again.

The Holy Spirit.

Remember.

You are cloaked in the grace of God. Inside and out.

She began to pray.

Silently, in the depth of her heart.

Slowly she realized she really was going to be okay just like her husband said. She had obviously been in a coma in the real world, but in her heart she had been at Milkweed Manor. And now, wonder of wonders, she had been given a second chance at life and she was going to savor every moment. Every. Single. Moment.

"Pardon?" said her husband. "Did you really say Kirby? Who is Kirby? And did you just wink?"

Oops. No way was she going to explain how she'd been living with caterpillars and butterflies, at least in her gut. No one would believe her. It had been her reality—at least in her dream state—but just too darn preposterous for others to comprehend.

"Oh, it's nothing. Just a bit mixed up, and no, I didn't wink. I think I have something in my eye," she said quickly, rubbing it, not wanting her family to know she had been winking at a butterfly. She could possibly be put away in the psych ward in no time if she started rambling about how she was a 'caterpillar-whisperer' and lived and ate dinner with them, as well as royal butterflies. If they thought it was strange a caterpillar and butterfly were hanging around, her actual truth would not be perceived well at all.

She looked around at her husband, daughter and son. Growing calmer by the moment, her heart exploded with love. Again. Blessed, glorious love. Always love, as Kirby and the queen would say.

"So wonderful to be back," she gushed. "So wonderful to see you."

This time she really observed each one of them, trying to take them in, literally drinking in their faces.

Her husband appeared exhausted but happy, as tears continued to leak down his cheeks. Her son looked pale and worried and her daughter seemed as if she might keel right over. Both of them dripped tears, as well. But they all had one thing in common... over their apparent shock, they appeared as thrilled to see her as she did them.

Oh, thank goodness.

"Group hug?" she asked, holding out her arms.

All of them leaned in and she held them close, not wanting to let them go, loving them with all her being.

The words of Saint Paul rang out in her heart.

Three things will last forever—faith, hope, and love—and the greatest of these is love.

Interesting how she now remembered those Bible passages exactly when she needed to. She even remembered the chapter and verse, courtesy of memorizing for religion class tests. 1Corinthian 13:13. It spoke of the power of love which she was now a huge believer in. It was definitely what life was all about and it took her forty-two years and a coma/stay at Milkweed Manor to discover it.

Holding her family close in her arms she knew she had, with the grace of God, changed. Forever. Like Saint Paul. She could feel it. She was committed to a better way of living. Oh, not that she was comparing herself to the glorious Saint Paul, but he was definitely a powerful role model and a reminder that people can really change. With God's divine power.

No longer would she live her life immersed in fears and anxieties, losing track of what was important in life.

All the cheesy Valentine commercials and Hallmark movies she loved so much were, in fact, true.

It was love. All about love.

Love of God. Love of self. Love of others.

And living in the present moment.

Always.

Fifteen

A Few Days Later

"Hey honey. Do you really think you are ready to do this?" asked Scott, wrapping his arms around Jenna and hugging her tightly. "You don't have to go, you know."

Jenna threw her arms around him just as tight. She enjoyed hugs but most of all loved her husband's support, enriched since her hospital stay. After a few moments of savoring his touch, she pulled back to gaze into his eyes.

They sparkled with love.

She sparkled right back.

Sometimes a crisis can expose weaknesses and irrevocably drive a marriage apart. Instead, they had grown closer, deepening their love that had once seemed to have drifted away.

She was lucky.

"I'm ready," she said. "I need to do this. To see how I feel when I'm there working. It was once my dream. I want to see if it still is."

Yes, she was going back to work for the very first time since her coma experience.

Jenna had discovered she never really did lose her job, or at least yet. Yet being the operative word. Guess her boss felt guilty for making promises and not keeping them, thrusting her into depression, leading to a fall and eventually a coma. Or apparently that was what he told Scott. He also said she still had a job which was certainly not what he had relayed to her the last time she had seen him. Guess he didn't want to look like the bad guy.

Not that she could blame her fall on Mr. Hull.

Sure she had been depressed, but she was the one who had brazenly stood on the deck railing searching for the caterpillar, lost her balance and tumbled off. How silly that she figured her gymnastic days from her teen years would keep her up there in the air. For one thing, she was a good fifty pounds heavier since then.

Turned out that fall was the best thing that had ever happened to her. Who would have guessed?

But job or no job, she still hadn't decided if she wanted to work with the firm anymore, even if she was kept on. The wisdom she had garnered at Milkweed Manor had her looking at life differently, so being at the office would help make her decision by uncovering the truth. Her feelings were mixed...part of her wanted to work for Mr. Hull, for it was what she was used to as well as a dream she'd once had, but another part wanted to leave, to stand up for herself, to walk away from a job that was rendered toxic when he decided to renege on his offer of partnership.

Not to mention the obvious toll it had taken on her family.

Time, and her heart, would tell.

"Well, I wish you all sorts of luck and courage and strength. And discernment."

"Thank you."

"Remember. I'm rooting for you all the way, no matter what your decision is."

"I know and I appreciate that."

She pulled on her coat.

"Love you," she said, kissing him goodbye.

"Love you back."

She walked out the door and into her SUV, stopping for a coffee on the way to her office. Usually she'd grab a chocolate chip muffin, sometimes two, even adding a donut, but she didn't want to be in some kind of food stupor at work. She needed to keep fully alert, not on a sugar high.

She smiled, thrilled she was choosing to feel good rather than stuff her feelings away, usually causing heartburn and a date with antacids. Not to mention self-loathing.

On the whole, it was choosing to respect herself. It was a practice she was trying to adhere to, sometimes tough, sometimes easy.

As she parked her car behind her office building, she took a few minutes to center herself, something she'd been doing since leaving the hospital.

The hospital.

She still couldn't compute that she had been in a coma, when all along she thought she was at Milkweed Manor learning lessons to last a lifetime. Then again, she often thought it was a dream, so a coma did make sense. It was really just being in a deep dream state with the noises of the machines that surrounded her, keeping her alive. After all, a world inhabited with giant talking caterpillars and butterflies could only exist in one's imagination, but her memory still presented fuzzy lines between her imagination and reality, for the wisdom she'd learned was guaranteed to last a lifetime. Knowledge that made total sense. Lessons to live by forever.

Once she had emerged, doctors were amazed that she seemed totally fine. Radiant even. All her stats in terms of blood pressure, pulse and CT scans proved she was one hundred percent okay. She was given a completely clean bill of health and released the next day. At her family's insistence, she took a few days off to be sure of her well-being, but emotionally she had never felt better. She was peaceful, happy and enjoying every moment of being with her family, also realizing she needed to implement a lot of changes in her own life, spurred on by the knowledge of the caterpillars and of course the king and queen. However, for now, she was just riding it out, living day to day, second to second.

And praying.

Yes, she was praying lots and she'd even dug out her old Bible to learn more about God, the Holy Spirit and the gift of grace. And of course...living in the present trusting that God would watch over her.

She was also trying to stay in tune with her family by observing, listening and loving them.

"Don't try to change others," advised the queen when Jenna hugged her goodbye. *"Just be your authentic real self and allow life to happen."*

The queen.

She couldn't get this beautiful butterfly out of her mind.

At first, she had been really confused over all the memories of the Manor that seemed to tumble around her. Especially the visits to her family where she saw problems she never knew existed.

Did she always know deep down what was going on but refused to face it?

Had they lingered in her, festered, and it all came out in the coma state?

She had no viable answers and even considered seeing a psychotherapist, and still might do so, but believed they'd simply tell her it really was her subconscious that saw all and rose up after her fall. Maybe so, however she still looked upon her stay in the Manor as a beautiful, life changing occurrence and continued to keep it quiet. She didn't want anyone marring the lovely chain of events she had experienced and eventually came to the conclusion that whatever it was, she had learned so much and it had made a huge difference in her life, so it was all good.

Not a nightmare in the least...in fact, a positive chapter in her world, fantasy or not.

After all, when she told people she'd been in a coma, many asked if she'd seen a bright light or heaven. She just smiled and said no. How could she explain that what she witnessed were giant caterpillars and butterflies who talked and lived the way she wished she could...in the present, in love, support and peace, honoring God, a higher being, nature, a source, or whatever they chose. These creatures never ever even came up in all the many books written about heaven or life ever after.

But it was definitely a challenge.

She was striving to live a life centered in the present, in a world where few shared her view. Or at least people in her immediate circle. She did manage, through scouring the internet, to find a few groups who shared her new view of life and really lived it, not just gave lip service to it, which was incredibly comforting and soothing to her soul. Eventually she hoped to find a mentor to help her along this incredible path. She felt the need for a butterfly guide to keep her focused. In human form, of course.

But she still didn't know if her children had the problems she'd witnessed in her coma state.

Yes, she had taken her son out for a haircut and bought him some new clothes. But he still insisted he loved basketball. And as for her daughter, she was eating lots and wearing baggy clothes and claiming life was good. Walking by the washroom many times when her daughter was in there yielded nothing.

Guess only time would tell.

And then there was her job.

Today held a great challenge.

To face her law career, having changed. Also, having 'grace/ wisdom' on her side.

She wondered how it would go?

What she would 'see?'

She'd had many discussions with Scott over whether to stay or quit. He'd even made a beautiful wooden shingle with her name painted on it in bold black letters, in case she wanted to open a law practice at their home, something she was considering.

But she needed to go back to the job she once loved, the job that claimed her almost twenty-four/seven, to figure it out.

Sucking in a deep cleansing breath and pushing it out again, she finally got out of the car, threw her shoulders back and walked tall and confident into the building and up to her boss's office.

"Great to see you," said Sandy, the head secretary at the firm. "Mr. Hull said to go right in."

"Thank you." She paused. "And hey, I know I've never really said this before, but thank you for all the hard work you do for us. This firm runs smoothly mainly because of you. You're efficient, kind, and know just as much about the law as we do. I appreciate you enormously."

Sandy opened her mouth in shock and Jenna felt bad that she had never taken the time to show her gratefulness. Oh sure, she gave the token Christmas present, even remembered her birthday, but it was not the same as sincere words acknowledging her special gifts. It was long overdue.

"Um, well, thank you, Jenna."

And she actually blushed.

"Well, I really mean it."

Sandy grinned just as the intercom buzzed.

"Is that Jenna out there?" barked Mr. Hull.

"Er, yes, sir."

"Send her in."

Jenna was struck by how impatient he sounded.

Had he always been like that?

Acknowledging how nervous she was, praying for strength, she walked over and stood at the door of his office.

"Come in, come in," he said, motioning to the chair in front of his desk, phone to his ear, obviously talking to someone, or shouting, was more like it.

She sat, paying close attention to how she felt, keeping in touch with her inner self, gleaning its wisdom.

For one thing, the hurt and anger she'd felt about their last conversation had mostly dissipated; however, it truly showed who he was, and caused her to be leery. If he treated valuable hard-working employees like he did her, disposing when convenient to him, he was someone to watch out for.

She simply didn't trust him.

Wow.

She had never realized that.

Had she always felt that way?

Bet she had, but simply suppressed her feelings as usual.

She didn't trust his son either, who apparently hadn't arrived yet. And she still wasn't sure she'd have a job as time marched on.

"Glad you're back," he said, finally putting his phone down. "Hope you are ready to start working again."

"Yes, I am," she said, pulling herself out of her thoughts. She smiled, then quickly sobered up when she noticed the stack of papers piled high on a table behind his desk.

Had he done nothing since she left?

Most important, was he expecting her to do all that? To catch up?

Another thing, now that she was back in his presence, she noticed how brusque he was and how it was all about the work. He had yet to even ask her how she was feeling, although Scott had said he had blamed himself. Or were those just the words he felt he had to say to her husband when he heard she was in the hospital? Fake words, not meaning them? Words to get him off the hook?

Was she just a work horse for him?

Someone to use?

To manipulate?

She felt guilty thinking such thoughts about him. After all, he had once been someone she respected. But in fact, it really wasn't about him. She just felt she was seeing things clearly for a change, which would influence her decisions.

It was all about her for now.

All about what was the next step in her life, what gave her the most peace.

"Good," he said, pulling her out of her thoughts. "We have a lot of contracts and paperwork to plow through." He wheeled his chair back and pointed to the pile. "I really need help here."

So he really had stockpiled her work until she came back.

"I'm ready." Maybe? "I'll get right to it."

Interesting. He still didn't seem concerned about her well-being and even whether she could handle a full schedule of work. He sure didn't want to talk about her coma, that was for sure. Guilt? Or just couldn't care less?

Good to note. Maybe she had always just been so grateful for a job that she ignored his dark side.

The phone rang and he picked it up, basically dismissing her. Jenna carried the heavy pile of papers back to her own office, hung up her coat, looked around briefly, then started right to work. As usual. Most of the papers required full-out checks to make sure they were in order and the simple filling out of names and addresses and needed signatures. It was familiar and safe and she could do this in her sleep, but after about twenty of them, she started to lose all concentration.

What was even stranger was that every few minutes, she found herself glancing up to stare at a picture of her family sitting on her desk.

The photo had been taken last Christmas.

Everyone had big, wide smiles on their faces.

She had loved the photo and considered it a real-life depiction of the loves of her life, therefore had it blown up and framed, proud to show it off. Now, with her newly found knowledge, she realized no one looked happy. Not even one of them, herself included. Oh, on the surface they did, and back then, she was really into seeing what she wanted to be there, not the truth. Now, she could plainly see the empty eyes and the sadness lurking behind the contrived smiles.

In fact, if it was placed at an art show, it would be titled - *Study in Sadness* or *Fake Smiles* or *Let's Pretend.*

"How blind I was last year."

Oops, had she said that out loud?

Guess so, for all of a sudden a butterfly soared out of nowhere and landed right on the picture.

As if agreeing with her assessment. Underlining it, so to speak.

Really?

She looked closely, amused.

"Hello, Kirby."

He didn't answer. In this world he didn't talk. She was never really sure it was her buddy at all, realizing not all monarchs could be him, until she saw the blue eyes. They were a dead giveaway. Then again, most butterflies wouldn't be hanging around a lawyer's office, so guessing it was him would most likely be almost one hundred percent correct.

It *had* to be her friend.

She leaned closer, observing him watching her intently, and immediately felt this beautiful creature was trying to tell her something.

She stared, he winked. He moved his legs.

Get out!

Was he dancing?

Their special happy dance?

She believed he was.

It was a sign. A sign of joy.

She stood, losing herself in the moment, swinging her feet and arms around, joining in their dance of life and hope and peace and just plain old fun.

It was truly glorious.

Finally, he stopped, landing on her hand.

"What is it, Kirby?"

They locked eyes.

Peace descended upon her.

She sat back down and immediately shifted back away from her muddled mind, observing her work life from afar.

Time to reflect.

Yes, she loved working as a lawyer.

However, she could see clearly how she was always going strong, a real work horse, right around the clock, incredibly dedicated, to the detriment of everything and everyone else. Even when surrounded by her family, she thought about work. She bet she had jumped up after that photo was taken to check her phone to see if Hull was trying to get hold of her. It was a fast-paced, overloaded job that left her very little time for anything else. Her lifestyle had been a race course surrounded by a mound of paperwork and courtroom drama, taking precedence over caring for herself and her loved ones.

She stared again at the photo.

Kind of looked like Kirby was staring at it too, by the way he was positioned on the frame facing it.

Sigh.

Her husband and children had gotten lost in her day to day life. She was beginning to know herself again, but sure didn't know them anymore.

She closed her eyes and imagined another photo.

One where smiles were real and love was evident.

She wanted that. She wanted to 'happy dance' with her husband and children and believed it was attainable.

Aha.

Her eyes popped open.

"Hey, Kirby. I know what you're trying to tell me."

She got it.

She pushed away from the desk.

She also knew what she had to do.

Being back in this office was a crossroads.

A test of her new self. Her authentic self.

Lost for so long, she realized she had continued on the path she once shared with her own mother, where work was piled on her shoulders, she felt alone, and what she wanted or needed was ignored. It was familiar territory. She was just carrying on the legacy.

Nope.

Not anymore.

Dream, coma or not, she had learned too much at the Manor.

She knew which way to go. Ahead, not backwards.

She reached her hand out and Kirby landed on her palm.

"Thank you, my friend. Thank you for your support and for helping me sort out a few things."

He winked. She winked back. He flew away. His job was done. Hers had just begun.

She stood up, took a deep breath, picked up the pile of paper and marched into Mr. Hull's office.

Luckily, he was there. She smiled. It would have been a shame to not have been able to act on her new-found courage.

"I quit," she said firmly.

"What?" He looked shocked. "But I worked hard to get my son to keep you on. You have a job here forever."

Oh? Funny how he never told her this or even made an attempt to reassure her. Too late, though. She'd made up her mind.

"Thank you, sir. But being back here helped me make my decision. It's family first. I can't keep up this workload and still find time to be with my husband and children. Just want you to know I thank you for employing me all these years, but I am leaving now."

She placed the contracts on his desk.

He started to protest but she just grinned and, following the queen's advice, *when need be, walk away.*

She did.

In fact, she ran.

She'd been loyal to him, definitely a hard worker, and she didn't want to stay and do battle over how or why she was leaving. Especially since he'd been so quick to let her go before her coma state, not to mention all the work he used to pile on, knowing she had a family. She wanted to honor herself, her authentic, real self, and sitting at her desk showed her how important it was to take care of herself. Only then could she truly care for her loved ones. It was as simple and as profound as that.

She needed to go.

No way could she allow the next Christmas photo taken to be fake.

Not if she could help it.

Jenna headed back to her office, gathered up her coat, purse and briefcase, said goodbye to a shocked Sandy who had obviously already been told she was leaving, and walked out the door, head held high. Getting into the car, she called her husband.

"Sooo, have you finished my shingle yet?" she asked.

"Almost," he said. Pause. "Will you be using it?"

"Yes."

"Good for you."

"I have another idea."

She quickly explained her thoughts, enjoyed the fact he agreed with her, still smiling as she hung up. In keeping with what they had discussed, she had one more stop to make. She turned left, then right, and arrived in the parking lot of the local humane society.

Last night, always wanting a dog, especially Ellie, they had gone there as a family to take a look. They had all fallen in love with a tiny Havanese puppy named Sparky, who had been dropped off by an owner who could no longer care for her. They didn't bring her home, for they still hadn't worked out the details of how to take care of a dog, seeing as they were all gone for the day.

She had sure solved that problem.

Jenna got out of the car, walked into the building and straight to the cage holding the little black dog.

She looked in. The tiny pup ran over to meet her, tail wagging, yipping excitedly.

"Come here, Sparky." She reached in to pat her head, a tear sliding down her cheek.

"You're coming home with me. To your forever home."

Jenna opened the crate door, and Sparky jumped into her arms, licking her face.

Best decision ever.

<h1 style="text-align:center">Sixteen</h1>

"Here we are."

Jenna opened the door to the house and held it for the little dog to enter.

"Everyone will be home soon and I'm sure you'll remember them from last night. Especially Ellie. She cuddled you the whole time we were there. She's going to be thrilled."

Sparky trotted in, still wagging her tail, acknowledging her joyful words as if she understood them. Jenna bet she did. In fact, she had never stopped wagging the whole way there. She was one happy dog and Jenna was one happy human. Completely delighted. After all, dogs were all about love and showing affection. She hoped Sparky would put smiles on her children's faces and help draw them all closer together as they cared for the newest addition to their family.

She was sure of it.

Getting a dog was a dream come true for Ellie and Jason.

Maybe? Hopefully?

Obviously on a sniffing mission, scouting out her new digs, Sparky roamed around until Jenna eventually led her to the kitchen. She had made a quick stop for dog food and bowls, filled them, and placed them on the floor. Sparky ran to them fast, her sense of smell working fine, chowing down, slurping water, back and forth, back and forth, almost not sure which bowl to finish first. Jenna watched her a while, lost in the enjoyment of puppy love.

"You're so darn cute," she said.

Oops. She had forgotten one more thing.

"Be right back."

She hurried out to the car to bring in the two pizzas she'd also stopped to pick up. She was greeted at the door by Sparky, thrilled to see her, even though she'd only been gone two minutes.

"This is what I love about dogs," she said, reaching down to give her a pet. "They are always glad to see you. But hey, I'd almost forgotten the people food."

Get a grip.

She walked out to the kitchen, Sparky following her, where she placed the food in the oven to keep warm. After laying out plates and napkins on the table, she was all ready to greet her children with their new pet. A surprise she was sure they'd love.

As if agreeing with her, she heard the front door slam, signaling they were home.

"Sparky, they're here, they're here."

The little dog cavorted, obviously influenced by her excited tone, twirling around, chasing her tail.

"Pizza?" asked Jason, racing into the kitchen. "I could smell it the moment I walked in." He opened the oven door. "Good. You remembered to get extra pepperoni."

"Sure did." From then on she was paying attention. Extra pepperoni it was. "And extra pineapple on the other one for Ellie. Lucky your dad and I don't care."

Jenna's eyes were once again on the dog, watching her perk up at the new arrival. Jason hadn't noticed her yet.

"Pizza?" shouted Ellie. "Yayyyyy..."

Sparky, obviously recognizing her voice, erupted into a high-pitched slew of yips and yaps and waddled over as fast as she could to greet Ellie, tail wagging so hard it threatened to fall off.

"Are you kidding me?" screamed Ellie, skidding to a stop. "We have a dog?"

She dropped to her knees, instant tears streaming down her cheeks as she wrapped her arms around the pup.

"No way. Is this Sparky? The same pup from last night?"

"Yes, it is," said Scott, arriving next and who had been in on the surprise. He smiled over at Jenna. His eyes were warm, clearly as touched as she was at their daughter's excitement.

"But how will we take care of her during the day?" asked Jason. "We can't leave her alone all by herself for hours and hours."

Sensitive, practical Jason. She loved how his mind worked, actually a lot like hers.

"Don't worry. Your father and I have a plan, but come on," said Jenna. "We don't want the pizza getting cold and we can chat while we eat."

She took them out of the oven and plopped them on the table.

Scott picked up a tray sitting on the counter and held it up.

"All cellphones go in here until dinner is over," he said firmly.

Surprised, they all handed them over, no arguments whatsoever. But that was probably because Sparky was distracting them.

When discussing their family life a few days earlier, Scott and Jenna had decided this was best. Scott, who was working on the same cell phone issues with his students at work, trying to stop them from bringing them to classes, had jumped in with this idea. Surprisingly he felt a lot like Jenna did, that their meal times were stressful and not community based and supportive. Too bad they hadn't discussed that ages ago.

"I thought I'd lost you the day I found you lying on the ground," he'd said. *"We need to be there for one another and really talk to each other. Somehow we've gotten our priorities confused."*

Jenna couldn't agree more.

Sure seemed as if, while she was staying at Milkweed Manor, Scott has also been on his own journey, reflecting on their lives together. He was eager to make changes that would bring them closer together. She was thrilled. It was not just all up to her and she rejoiced that she had a partner in her new way of life. Almost a Kirby in human form. Once again, for about the tenth time since emerging from her coma, she realized how lucky she was.

Today was the first time he'd implemented the phone rule, however.

Great.

No protests yet. Maybe it really was the distraction of the dog, or a result of her landing in the hospital which had challenged all of them, bringing them closer.

"Um, may I eat my pizza on the floor?" asked Ellie. "To keep Sparky company?"

Eyebrows raised, Scott glanced at Jenna, and she nodded her approval.

"Sure," said Scott. "Or how about you sit with us and hold her on your lap."

Jenna knew he probably didn't like the idea of a dog sitting with them at the table but was obviously making an exception, noting how excited Ellie was and wanting her to be part of their family community. She was amazed as well at how closely her daughter held onto the pup. Jason had barely even gotten in a pat on the head. The tiny dog was like Ellie's lifeline or something. Interesting to see, to note.

Jenna had been watching her children carefully since she left the hospital.

Originally, she'd wanted to rush in and demand to know if it all was true, asking Jason about basketball and Ellie about her eating habits. However, she knew that wasn't the way to handle matters for it might drive them further apart and she also wasn't sure if her findings at the Manor were real or imagined. So she just kept looking for signs of issues, worries and concerns.

Scott seemed in the dark about their children as well. Guess he'd been blind too. Add that to young people possibly being expert at hiding their troubles, and you have illusions but no facts.

Time for them to end. She craved truth.

Hopefully she'd figure it all out and soon. Especially if their daughter was bulimic. Now *that* was very serious.

But for now, she had the present moment. And for this she was eternally grateful. A moment of peace, a moment of observation, a moment of love, fun and laughter.

After chowing down on pizza, sipping sodas, and a round of general talk of how everyone's day went, Jenna decided it was time to share her news.

"I have an announcement to make," she burst out.

Ellie and Jason looked at her, obviously alarmed, judging by their raised eyebrows and worried looks.

"Don't be anxious. It's good news. I have decided to open up my own law practice right here at home."

"Really?" asked Ellie. "Are you going to work two jobs now?"

"No. I resigned from my position at Hull's."

"But I thought you loved it there," said Jason.

"I did but I love my family even more. I'm reducing my work load and practicing at home by making the den into my office. I am hoping to be less stressed and able to help you more. This way you'll never have to worry about rides to games or extracurricular activities. I'll be available to take you."

"Oh, so you can watch Sparky throughout the day, too?" asked Jason.

"Yes."

He looked relieved.

"Good."

"So what do you think, Ellie?" she asked.

"I think it's wonderful," said Ellie, her eyes lighting up. "This way you'll be calmer and not freak out over every little thing."

True words, but they still hurt.

But really, was I that stressed out and erratic when I worked? thought Jenna.

She looked around, studying their facial expressions.

Ellie looked happy, sporting a wide grin. Jason still seemed relieved, obviously having been worried about their new dog, and Scott wore a smile that would give the Cheshire cat a run for who had the biggest grin ever.

Of course, she was *that* stressed and they all knew it.

She was kidding herself if she thought anything else.

But still, the calmer faces on her children and husband really sliced through her heart. She was glad, but found it still hard to face the fact the constant ball of worry that ruled her had hurt her family so badly.

Don't dwell on that.

It would be allowing the past to clutter her moment, where she was thrilled to have this second chance of being with her family. Instead, she wanted to treasure every second.

But since she was still seeking truth, she decided to speak more of her mind. She was on a searching mission.

"So enough of me," said Jenna, pouring drinks, looking around the table. Who should she tackle first? "How is basketball, Jason?"

"Okay." He shrugged and grabbed another slice of pizza.

Was it really okay?

Or were his words a fake job?

Was the fact he grabbed more pizza at that moment a cover-up? Was he stuffing food down his throat like she did? To avoid facing real feelings?

She had to know.

In the Manor, she had often wondered if she had pressured him to play this sport, one *she* loved, for she did recall his lack of enthusiasm for his games. Of course, then she heard it for herself when she visited the house. But as she had mentioned, she wasn't sure if everything she witnessed while in her own chrysalis was true. But he was a lot like her, just grinning and bearing things. Putting up with something so as not to make waves or bother others, especially her. She had to find out for real what he thought. She wasn't going to let the subject drop, like the old days where she ran from problems.

"Do you enjoy playing basketball?" Time to push and bring this out to the light.

He looked startled.

"Um, I guess."

Ellie cleared her throat and Jenna watched them exchange a sharp look.

Interesting.

She leaned closer, watching him.

"Well, you know…" She smiled warmly, searching for the right words. "The other day I caught you dancing around in the kitchen. Hip hop, I guess you call it."

He turned red.

"Well, um, it was just that a good song came on. I didn't know you were watching."

"It was an honor. You are pretty amazing and you look incredibly talented, as well. You sure know some moves. Come to think of it, you always loved to dance when you were little, often imitating dancers you saw on YouTube. I was wondering, would you rather do that instead of basketball?"

Did his eyes actually light up?

She stared. Yes, they had.

Jason completely stopped eating and stared.

"You really mean it? You mean I could quit basketball and take up dancing lessons? At the Blue Moon?"

"Of course you can."

How had she forgotten how he used to stare longingly in the door of the Blue Moon Dance Studio when they walked by on the way to the grocery store. Not to mention he was always shuffling around his feet, spinning and moving. How had she missed all that? Ignored it all? Especially since Scott had done the same. Her husband loved to dance, too. Always grabbing her for a waltz in the kitchen or living room. Or at least he used to.

She continued to watch as Jason glanced at his sister again, eyebrows raised, still surprised. She saw Ellie give him a little nod. He turned back.

"Really? You honestly mean it?"

"Yes," added Scott, jumping in, agreeing. "We will both support you in whatever you want to do."

"Well, okay then." His excited voice rose in pitch. "Yeah, to be honest, I'm not too crazy about basketball, but I'd love to take hip hop lessons. I even have saved birthday money to pay for them. I could start now but I think I will continue basketball. We only have two games left and I wouldn't want to let the team down."

"Great," said Jenna. "Maybe we can pop over to the dance studio after dinner and get you signed up."

"All right." He picked up his slice of pizza and bit into it, eyes glowing, feet moving, barely able to contain himself.

Joy suffused her heart.

She pushed away her old thoughts of how she had been such a lousy mother, not knowing her son, and instead was thrilled she had helped put that sparkle back in her son's eyes.

Thank you, Milkweed Manor. Thank you so much for all I learned there.

"I am thrilled you are happy about this, Jason," she said. "And I am truly sorry that I pressured you into playing a sport you didn't like." She looked around the table. "Please, Jason, Ellie. Please feel free to come to me and/or your father if you need help or want to talk about anything. I know I have been stressed and over busy for years but that has ended. I just want you both to be happy. To follow your dreams."

Once more she watched Jason lock eyes with Ellie. She remembered their pinky-swear pact, the one she witnessed at this very same table. The agreement that if Jason told her that he didn't want to play basketball, Ellie would reveal her eating disorder. She hoped and prayed that more secrets would be uncovered, if any, and harmony would flow in. She was counting on it.

So far, her daughter wasn't talking. Hopefully soon. Really, soon.

They finished the pizza with much laughter, joy, excitement, along with discussions about Sparky, for instance, deciding who would walk her, feed her and so on. Eventually, Scott excused himself to do some paperwork and Jason ran to get ready for a visit to the dance studio.

"Look how cute she is," said Ellie, placing Sparky down on the floor, watching her circle around and around chasing her tail.

Obviously, judging from her previous play before supper, something she loved to do. "Did they tell you how old she is?"

"Two months," said Jenna. "Her previous owner got a new job, had to move away and didn't feel he could take the dog overseas."

"Lucky us," said Ellie, beginning to teach the tiny dog how to 'shake a paw'. She looked up. "Hey, can I take dog lessons at Tina's Obedience School? Rather than tennis lessons? I would love to teach Sparky some tricks and stuff and I have lots of babysitting money saved."

"Yes, of course."

How easier life was when her children felt free to speak up, knowing they would be listened to. How happier it made everyone. How simpler.

Jenna was also touched by her daughter's love for the little pup, but still very worried about her weight loss.

She was watching and listening, still trying to decide when to jump in.

She hoped that rather than plowing into Ellie's life with her own agenda, her daughter would trust her with the truth.

Soon.

Really soon.

Seventeen

Two weeks later

"Jenna. There is someone here to see you," shouted Scott.

"Sure, honey. I'll be down in a minute."

She wasn't expecting a visitor and wondered who it could be.
Maybe a new client?

Much to her surprise, her business had boomed fast. She was
fortunate, because she was already well known in her small town and
clients were arriving daily. She had been thoroughly enjoying working
on her own, selecting cases she believed in and supported, helping
people who genuinely needed her expertise in matters of the law. She
was also thrilled to announce she was looking into more studies and
a commitment to environmental law. Milkweed Manor renewed her
love of all nature and she wanted to do her part in conserving and
taking care of the world, the best she could. It was another dream of
hers that had gotten lost along the way and was being resurrected. She
felt good about that.

So even in this short while, she found herself smiling lots, was
less stressed and able to give more to herself and her family. It really

was true. The more she loved and cared for herself, striving to live in authenticity, the more she had to give to others. And to think she once believed it selfish to think of her own needs.

Jenna was also continuing to live in the present, or at least practicing doing so. She didn't always achieve it but life was sure more peaceful than before. She had to admit though, that she often felt lost. She was changing old patterns and habits and introducing a new way of life and many times she felt shaken in her quest to do so. Unsure of who she was. However, her ability to continue to really see matters as they were, clearly, and not through the crippling haze of worry and fear, past and future anxieties, changed her and definitely for the better. So she was continuing to grow in the new 'you' state, trying to live her real self.

Oops.

Better get a move on. Enough musing for now. For in her 'present' moment, she apparently had a visitor.

She took off fast down the stairs.

"Where are you?" she called out.

"We're in the kitchen," shouted her husband.

Jenna walked in to find Scott and the children sitting around the kitchen table with a woman she didn't know. Sparky was curled up in Ellie's arms gazing at her adoringly, as per usual. They were rarely apart.

"This is Ms. Papillon," said her husband. "Apparently she took care of you at the hospital. We never managed to meet because I guess she was there during the night when we left to grab a nap, shower or change clothes. She came today to pay you a visit."

"Nice to meet you."

Jenna reached her hand out for a shake and when they touched, she felt a jolt, like an electric shock. She stared at the lady, startled.

She knew those eyes.

She'd looked into them before.

But when? Where? Her memory drew a blank.

"Take a seat," said her husband, pulling out her chair.

She sat, hands in her lap, still gazing at the lady.

Ms. Papillon smiled. "I hope you don't mind me visiting. It's part of our hospital protocol aftercare program to check in with coma patients to see how they're faring."

"Well, thank you for caring. In fact, I'm doing great."

Her coma.

Yeah, right.

Somehow this still made her giggle. For in the eyes of her family, she was in a coma for three days, but in her reality she was at Milkweed Manor for months. At times she still felt like bursting out and sharing her story of butterflies and caterpillars and telling everyone the glorious lessons she had learned. But nope, she still kept it her secret, believing no one would understand her thoughts. Sometimes, she didn't either. All she knew was that it had changed her, for the better and forever. But it still amused her thinking of how people would react if they knew how much she had learned from living with those glorious creatures.

Then again, maybe it really wasn't too strange.

For instance, if someone into computers dreamed about computers, it would make sense. Or a teacher dreaming about students, or a dog lover dreaming about dogs. She truly did love nature and all its creatures, even though she had shoved her love away, so dreaming about the beauty of the earth and the butterflies she loved was not really a stretch.

So maybe one day, she really would tell her story.

And it was still amazing that she had a butterfly with blue eyes who followed her around helping her.

Or at least she believed he helped her.

She checked out the curtains. Yep, Kirby was there. As always. Her family still freaked out about that, but to her it was truly glorious.

"She's amazing," interjected her husband. "She seems to have come out of that state a much happier person."

Jason and Ellie nodded their agreement.

"So you feel better?" asked Ms. Papillon.

"Sure do," said Jenna. "Much more clear-headed and focused."

"When do you go back to work?"

"Well, I'm already there. I made a lot of changes and I'm proud to say I opened up my own business. Right here at home."

"Really? And this works out well for you?"

"Sure does."

At that moment, Kirby flew over and landed on her hand. She looked at him.

Once again, he winked. Every time he did that, a shot of serenity washed through her. He was her constant reminder that she had evolved.

"I see you have a friend," said Ms. Papillon.

"Yes, I call him Kirby."

"It's a fun name and we tease her about it," said her husband. "But for some reason the butterfly keeps close to my wife, almost as if protecting her."

"How interesting." Ms. Papillon smiled. "But he does indeed look like a Kirby and I'm sure it's a sign of good things. And I'm pleased to see you are happier starting your own business and in general, with your life."

"Sure am. In terms of work, I can take whatever cases I want and still be here for my family. There is less pressure, making me happier in all areas of my life."

"How are the rest of you doing?" Ms. Papillon looked around the table.

"Well, I quit basketball," said Jason.

Jenna was surprised he spoke up, but then again, this lady radiated a soothing comforting presence that inspired conversation. It was quite a gift.

"And I never thought my mom would let me," continued a grinning Jason. "I take hip hop lessons now."

"So you love to dance?"

"Sure do."

"He used to dance for hours as a child," said Jenna. "I should have enrolled him in class years ago."

"And I have a dog," said Ellie, waving Sparky's paw in the air. "I've wanted one for ages."

"Yes, you do." Ms. Papillon leaned over to pat the pup's head. "Seems like you adore her and vice versa."

"Well, it's actually the family dog, but she always follows me around."

"Sure does," said Jenna. "It's sweet to see."

"So all seems to be going well."

"Yes," said Scott. "Almost losing my wife and my children their mother, made all of us rethink the way we'd been living. We are trying to communicate better and draw closer together."

Jenna was surprised at her husband. Usually he kept things to himself too, so to blurt out information voluntarily to a woman he didn't know was rather shocking. In fact, it was rather spectacular.

"And it appears to be working," added Jenna. "Life seems so much better, the way we all used to envision it."

"Good. It appears like you are going to be okay. Just wanted to make sure." She stood. "I'd better be going now."

Jenna jumped up, somehow sad to see this lady leave. Odd, since she'd only known her a few minutes.

"I'll walk you to the door."

"Thank you."

When they reached the entryway, Jenna said, "May I give you a hug?" She was surprised she said this for she wasn't in the habit of hugging strangers. But somehow, she felt the need.

"Of course. I would like that."

Ms. Papillon's arms wrapped around her.

Oh my goodness, they were familiar, comforting, like the... like the... queen.

She pulled back and stared at the woman.

Recognition flooded her heart.

She knew who this woman was. She knew those eyes, those arms, this presence of serenity.

She was the queen.

Her mentor at the Manor.

Her night nurse?

Had her soothing presence during her coma helped create the safe, warm place for her to grow? To face her fears? To heal?

Tears flooded her face.

Once again she thought that whatever happened back then turned out to be the best thing ever.

"I know who you are," she whispered. "And all I can say is thank you."

At that moment, Kirby flew over and landed on Ms. Papillon's shoulder. They winked in unison.

"You're welcome," said Ms. Papillon/the queen. "I'm so happy to see you smiling deeply, from the heart, and know that you are well. I also have a little gift for you."

She handed Jenna a small box, shockingly wrapped in her butterfly curtains.

Coincidence? *I think not.*

She opened it.

Inside was a gold chain with a tiny monarch butterfly clasped to it. Engraved on the underside of the butterfly were the words '*and the greatest of these is love.*'

"So you will always remember," said Ms. Papillon.

Jenna stared at her, confused by what was going on, but loving it all at the same time.

"May I come visit you?" asked Jenna. "Please?"

"Anytime. I will always hear the call of your heart."

What did she mean by that?

As the lady turned to leave, Kirby followed her out the door. He turned to give Jenna one last look, nodded his head, then continued on. Jenna had the feeling it would be the last time she saw him.

Eighteen

The next day, Jenna called the hospital.

No Ms. Papillon worked there.

Why was she not surprised?

She searched for her on the internet, even checked out images, but could find no lady who resembled the woman who had come into her house.

Her search did, however, lead her to a fact she never knew.

The word *papillon* was the French word meaning butterfly. It was also the name of a toy breed of dogs who had ears resembling butterfly wings.

How apt.

Jenna fingered the necklace.

The queen was right.

She could always visit her in her heart.

She had also guessed, but now knew, she would never see Kirby again. He was no longer flying around, near her at all times. She often felt sad about that, but guessed he, too, believed she could do it on her own. He had faith in her, and it was his time to soar away, probably to help someone else. She was just grateful for all the moments she'd had to spend with him, and felt happy that others would benefit from this beautiful creature.

She also remembered the words the queen had said, when they first met.

"Sometimes things just can't be explained," she said, *with a mysterious smile. "They are simply the way they are meant to be. The way our journeys lead us."*

She was right.

Her stay in Milkweed Manor just couldn't be explained.

But like she always said to herself over and over, it was the best thing that ever happened to her.

Like Saint Paul, it was her own personal road to Damascus, where she had met the risen Lord.

She had truly changed forever.

She was also reading the Bible daily, especially all about St. Paul, her hero. Her faith was growing and she had even made a poster of St. Paul's words in Ephesians, *"It is by grace that you are saved, through faith, not by anything of your own, but by a pure gift from God, and not by anything you have achieved. Nobody can claim the credit. You are God's work of art."*

The queen's faith in her, not to mention Kirby's complete trust in her, signaled she was ready to fly. She truly believed she was 'God's work of art.' Everyone was, and she wanted to live accordingly.

On her own.

Authentically.

Oh, there would be ups, there would downs, but she knew to keep trying, keep living, and most of keep loving. Always.

Day by day.

Striving to dwell in the present moment, pushing aside her past and future worries, stopping to smell the roses, as the old saying went.

She was ready.

Feeling peaceful, she settled down in her sunroom to meditate, loving the joy it created in her life, a true time of amity.

After about a half hour, she sensed someone enter the room.

Her eyes popped open.

"Mom, gotta moment?"

Jenna looked up to find Ellie there, as always holding Sparky.

"Sure. Anytime." She patted the couch beside her.

"Did you mean it when you said we could tell you anything?" asked Ellie, plopping down, Sparky curled in her lap.

"Yes, of course. Anything."

Silence.

Jenna waited her out, feeling that whatever was going on was incredibly important.

"Um, er, I have a problem." She cuddled Sparky, hugging her tightly as if for support.

"Yes?"

"Well, I... er... think I have an eating disorder."

So, the facts she'd discovered in her coma state really were true. Jenna figured she really did know them all along, but buried them deep, afraid to face the truth. Now, it was all out.

She reached out to hug her daughter.

Words weren't necessary. Her daughter needed a good old butterfly hug of comfort.

Ellie hesitated then wrapped her arms around her mother, sobbing.

"Are you mad at me, Mom?" she gasped out.

"No, of course not, honey. Thank you for sharing this."

"You suspected?"

"Yes, I did. But I waited for you to tell me. I know it wasn't easy and please know, no matter what, I love you with all my heart."

"But what if I hadn't told you?"

"Oh, don't worry. I would have come to you."

"And that would have been okay, too, Mom."

Jenna hugged her tighter.

"So how are you feeling?"

Ellie pulled back.

"Kinda horrible, really. Weak, shaky. Oh, Mom, I need help. I think I am bulimic."

Wow. Another score for the Manor. The fact she was bulimic was indeed the truth.

"Yes? Well, I'm here for you, dear. We'll get through this together."

Sparky leaned up to lick Ellie's face.

"All of us," added Jenna. "Sparky will help too."

"Will I get better?"

"Yes." There was no doubt in her heart, whatsoever. "Your family will be there every step of the way. But first we need to see a doctor."

Their second hug was deep and powerful, for this time Ellie reached out, craving comfort.

"Okay," said Ellie.

"I'll call right now."

Ellie pushed away, looked scared but nodded. "All right. It's time."

Jenna summoned up their doctor's number on her cell, phoned, and secured an appointment immediately due to the serious nature of the issue. Also, as luck had it, someone had just cancelled their appointment. Luck? No. Jenna was sure it was divine intervention. Happening, just when it was needed.

While Ellie took Sparky out for a potty break and then to change her clothes, Jenna used the brief opportunity to calm herself.

She acknowledged her fear for her daughter but knew they would all get through it and Ellie would finally receive the help she needed.

She liked this new way of living.

It was one of peace.

It was a lifetime commitment with many challenges.

But she had the tools to deal with it.

Step back. Observe her feelings. Pray for healing. Feel at peace but most of all, love yourself with all your heart which enabled you to love others with all your heart. And above all, live within your authenticity.

She picked up the phone to call her husband.

The queen and Kirby were right.

Love really was what it was all about.

And, of course, God.

For as St. Paul says, Love is patient, love is kind. It does not envy, it does not boast, it is not proud. It does not dishonor others, it is not self-seeking, it is not easily angered, it keeps no record of wrongs. Love does not delight in evil but rejoices with the truth. It always protects, always trusts, always hopes, always perseveres...*And now these three remain: faith, hope and love.*

And of course.

Jenna touched her butterfly necklace, recalling the words on the back.

The greatest of these is love.

Forever words to live by.

THE BEGINNING

Meet Suzanne Hurley

Happiness to this author is curling up with her laptop creating imaginary worlds that come from her heart. Writing is her passion and dreaming up story lines is her love. Suzanne was born in Peterborough, Ontario and currently resides in Caledonia, Haldimand County, where on morning walks with Rico, she tries out her new plots on the cows, sheep and numerous wild animals she greets along the way. Please visit Suzanne at her website:

http://suzannemhurley.blogspot.ca/

Other Works From The Pen Of
Suzanne M. Hurley

Samantha Barclay Mystery Series:

Changeable Facades - A murder has been committed! No one believes it but a young boy and his high school counselor. Will they catch the killers before he or she strikes again?

Delusions - Narcotics are sweeping Milton High! A student is dead! Lies and Deceit take over, as high school counselor Samantha Barclay is immersed in yet another deadly drama.

Chances – FBI Agent Ryan Leam's son is missing. Psychologist Samantha Barclay risks her life to go undercover at Sacred Heart Academy, seeking truth. The results are shocking and unbelievable.

Shades of Envy – Dead bodies are stacking up! Teenagers want to be vampires! The sheriff is acting secretively! Psychologist Samantha Barclay sets out on a wild ride to uncover the truth. Her discoveries lead to confrontations of the deadly kind. Will she survive with her life, as well as her heart intact?

Who did it? – Who killed the beloved principal of St. Michael's High School? Newly minted FBI agent Samantha Barclay's first case is to find the murderer. Only one problem. Everyone she meets has a reason to see him dead. Will she uncover who did it – before he or she strikes again?

Love? – Samantha Barclay discovers what people will do in the name of love, when a dead body is discovered in her basement and her beloved step-mother is arrested for murder.

Guilt – Who killed Doctor Ingrid Sayers? High school teacher David Harris says he did. Samantha Barclay disagrees and races against all odds to find the real murderer

The Cookie Club – One by one, the residents of Landon, West Virginia, are dropping dead. FBI/school psychologist Samantha Barclay, sets out to find the killer, before it becomes a ghost town.

Women's Fiction:

Nice Girls Can Win – Lawyer Jessie White is fired, evicted and jilted, all on the same day. Hitting rock bottom, she moves back home and immediately ends up in a sparring match with 'Red', the hunky guy next door. She soon discovers that miracles really do happen and how love often finds you, just when you're not looking.

Wings of the Past – Zoey Avery thinks she is happy, until wedding thoughts infiltrate her marriage-phobic mind. Only one problem – the groom she is dreaming about is a man she hasn't seen in thirteen years.

The Dream Smasher – Best-selling author Tracy Hazel is devastated to discover she is the victim of identity theft, when someone submits a horrid book, claiming she wrote it.

The Christmas Rose – Sparks fly, when Principal Olivia Lyons tries to uncover which student stole a million-dollar Christmas ornament. Her new guidance head thinks she did it. Will she end up in jail, love, or both?

Young Adult

The Teddy Bear Eye Club – Depressed, fourteen-year-old Mayah Lewis hides from the world, until she befriends new girl, beautiful bald-headed Celeste Daniels. Everything begins looking up, until one day, Celeste disappears.

Letter to Our Readers

Enjoy this book?

You can make a difference

As an independent publisher, Wings ePress, Inc. does not have the financial clout of the large New York Publishers. We can't afford large magazine spreads or subway posters to tell people about our quality books.

But, we do have something much more effective and powerful than ads. We have a large base of loyal readers.

Honest Reviews help bring the attention of new readers to our books.

If you enjoyed this book, we would appreciate it if you would spend a few minutes posting a review on the site where you purchased this book or on the Wings ePress, Inc. webpages at: https://wingsepress.com/

Visit Our Website

For The Full Inventory
Of Quality Books:

Wings ePress.Inc
https://wingsepress.com/

Quality trade paperbacks and downloads
in multiple formats,
in genres ranging from light romantic comedy
to general fiction and horror.
Wings has something for every reader's taste.
Visit the website, then bookmark it.
We add new titles each month!

Wings ePress Inc.
3000 N. Rock Road
Newton, KS 67114